Sabrina

So now…it is time to play…

By Scott M. Stockton

PublishAmerica
Baltimore

First printing

All characters in this book are fictitious, and any resemblance to real persons, living or dead, is coincidental.

PublishAmerica has allowed this work to remain exactly as the author intended, verbatim, without editorial input.

ISBN: 978-1-4489-8392-6

PUBLISHED BY PUBLISHAMERICA, LLLP

www.publishamerica.com

Baltimore

Printed in the United States of America

*This is for mom, my friends and family,
and Sam, and old friend.
"I couldn't have done it without your support"*

Sabrina

So now…it is time to play…

Prologue
January 3, 1987

The night was terrible. All over the city of Warren there was a strong icy blizzard bringing heavy amounts of snow. Cars had been stuck frequently throughout the day and schools were closed all over the entire county. It had been a tiresome day for many, except for one family. The LaMore family was among the wealthiest in the city. They lived in Unicorn Acres, and on this night of snow, there was a special and very memorable event. A child was born. Now, this was no ordinary child...she was rare. Mrs. Erika LaMore had named her daughter, Sabrina. A magnificent name for a magnificent child. Mr. Victor LaMore stood beside his wife as they held their precious baby, whom was born with jet black hair and the greenest eyes you'd ever seen. He had tears of joy, and they were happy that she was perfectly normal and healthy.

Part 1

When They Were Young

Chapter 1

It was a hot summer-like day in New York City, about 99 to 100 degrees. Clair was waiting for her best friend to get out of the bathroom. They had already been a few minutes late to catch the city bus and Clair didn't want to be late for school.

"Hillary, hurry up, we're going to be late!" she called.

"I'm coming" Hillary said as she ran down the staircase. She grabbed her backpack off the living room sofa. "Bye mom."

Clair Nelson and Hillary Dunn were both seventeen and had been friends for quite a while. Clair had long dark brown curly hair the matched her brown eyes. She also wore silver rimmed glasses and was very smart for her age. She always had perfect grades in school, and was able to speak Japanese well. Being sort of a perfectionist, she tended to want everything clean and organized. Her intelligence and confidence made her quite courageous; she never seemed to be afraid of anything. Hillary was like the exact opposite. She had short straight blonde hair and blue eyes. Hillary got average grades in school. She was sort of messy and unorganized, and wasn't brave like Clair. She was afraid of heights, small closed spaces and sharp objects. Her fear of sharp objects was due to an accident with a butcher knife, when she was four years old. Now, she has a large scar on her hand, which reminds her of the event.

"Why are we taking the bus to school today? Don't we usually ride in Alex's car? Hillary asked.

"We're taking the bus because Alex hit a stop sign while driving his mom to the store last night. His dad said it should be repaired by tomorrow" said Clair. Alex's car was a white 1989 Chrysler LeBaron convertible that he got for his sixteenth birthday form his grandparents. Clair and Hillary got on the bus and went toward the back where their boyfriends, Alex and Joshua were. Alex was Clair's boyfriend and Joshua was Hillary's boyfriend and they'd been together for over a year now.

"Hi Alex, hi Josh!" said Hillary with delight.

"What took you so long?" Joshua asked.

"Hillary had to go to the bathroom" said Clair in aggravation.

"Well, I had a lot of juice with breakfast this morning" Hillary added.

"Why did it have to be so hot today?!" Clair exclaimed. She took out a portable hand fan form her purse that ran by batteries and put it up to her face.

"It's because of the heat wave that came in from the south" said Alex as he opened the bus window beside him.

"Did you know that we're supposed to get a new student at school today?" Joshua asked, looking at his friends.

"No?" said Clair, questionably.

"I heard about that, she's supposed to come in during our math class, third period" Hillary added. Hillary was putting on eye blush while holding up a portable mirror.

"Well, who is she?" Clair asked.

"I don't know, but she's coming all the way from Warren, Pennsylvania" said Hillary.

"Where's Warren at in Pennsylvania?" asked Joshua.

"North of Pittsburgh and east of Erie" Clair explained.

"I wonder what this girl is like" Joshua said.

Joshua Deller and Alex Sanderson were also seventeen. Alex had short blonde hair and brown eyes. He was tall and he treated Clair like she was a queen. Joshua had had short brown hair and hazel eyes. He was an average height and mostly the quiet type.

When they all finally got to the high school after having a long sweaty ride on the city bus, Clair was suddenly upset.

"Remind me never to ride that disgusting bus ever again!" she yelled. "I got a glob of chewed gum on my skirt when I sat down on the seat!" All four teenagers walked over to their lockers. Clair pulled out a portable wet wipe from a package in her locker. She needed to wipe up the rest of the gum on her black skirt.

"You'd think the city buses would be cleaner then that" said Hillary to Clair.

"Not in New York" said Clair with a negative attitude.

When third period came around, Clair was in a better mood.

"I hope you didn't forget your math notes. Today is our test on percentages" said Clair to Alex. Hillary and Joshua were already in the classroom. Alex and Clair walked to the left side of the room near their friends. Their seats were by a long row of windows in the immense classroom. On the right side of the room, toward the back, sat Gloria Johnson and her other three friends: Brenda, Lorelei, and Harlene. Gloria had semi long red hair. She was sort of heavyset and she never passed her classes in school. Brenda Mainwell had light brown hair that was always kept up in a ponytail. Brenda often did not pass her classes, due to her lazy demeanor. Lorelei Daniels had dirty blonde hair and was somewhat more studious than her girlfriends. She had the tendency to pass some of her classes, but not many. Last of all, was Harlene Coleman, a candid, earthy young lady. She had long blonde hair and was somewhat quick-witted. She usually did well in academics, displaying a unique, notable style. She usually liked to be called Harley for short. These four teenage girls always picked on Clair and Hillary.

"Hey Clair, I see you're wearing that ugly black skirt again! You should really change your style. The skirt makes you look like shit!" laughed Gloria. Alex quickly got up out of his seat, ready to defend Clair.

"Alex, sit down, I'll handle it" said Clair calmly. She walked over to Gloria and spoke.

"Gloria, I don't talk to people that have a lower IQ than the average person. Which means, I will never talk to you, because you're too pointless to speak to!" Gloria humbly stopped smiling as Clair walked back to her seat. The teacher walked into the room abruptly, discouraging the gregarious bunch of teenagers.

"Good morning class. Today we have a new student. She is from Warren, Pennsylvania" said the teacher. A girl that was seventeen, maybe a year older, walked into the room tentatively. She had long, glossy, black hair that went down to her lower back. She was wearing a tight red dress with five bronze buttons going down the exterior. She had on tall black dress boots which went with her hair. She was holding a doll that was wearing a light blue dress and a large hat that covered the eyes. The doll had the same color hair as the girl, almost like her twin.

"Class, this is Sabrina LaMore, she will be joining our school for the rest of the year" said the teacher.

Gloria stared at Sabrina for a few minutes and then spoke.

"Why do you have a doll? Haven't you grown up yet?" Gloria asked, being cocky.

"Gloria Johnson do you have any consideration for people? I want you to go outside the room and wait for me to come and talk to you!" said the teacher.

"But, don't we have a test today?" asked Gloria.

"You can make it up tomorrow" the teacher said. Gloria flailed out of the room

"That's not very fair, Gloria was just asking a question!" said Harlene.

"Harlene, would you like to join Gloria out in the hall?" the teacher asked.

"No" replied Harlene.

"Well then I suggest you keep your mouth shut when I'm talking" said the teacher. Harlene rolled her eyes.

"Sorry about that, I'm Ms. Gladys Ribbons, it's nice to meet you" said the teacher. Ms. Ribbons had short brown hair and black rimmed glasses. She was tall, a bit old fashioned in appearance, a stereotypical looking teacher. She was usually very nice. She however, didn't like kids that were disrespectful or misbehaved in her class.

"Why don't you tell us why you do carry the doll, Sabrina" said Gladys. The girl looked at the class and then spoke.

"The doll's name is Clementine. I'm a Ventriloquist" said Sabrina slowly but clearly.

"Oh, how long have you had her? Did your parents give her to you?" Gladys asked. Sabrina's cat-green eyes darted toward the inquisitive instructor abruptly, as if Gladys had kicked her in the shin.

"You shouldn't ask so many questions, it's impolite" said

Clementine, in a moderate, childish voice. All the kids in the class where amazed at how Sabrina made the doll talk so smoothly.

"Ah...okay...um would you please sit at one of the empty desks at the back of the room" said Ms. Ribbons.

"Certainly" said Sabrina in a charming manner, as she walked toward the back. Sabrina sat behind a girl named Lynda Lark. Lynda loved to read. She was often in the school's library, studying and reading. Lynda was hoping to become a teacher herself one day.

"Okay class, I'm going to pass out the tests. I hope you all studied last night. The test mainly deals with percentages, but I put in some fraction problems too" said Ms. Ribbons. She handed everyone three worksheets that were stapled together.

"Try your best and take your time. You will have the whole class period to take your test. Sabrina, since you're new, you are not required to take the exam" said Ms. Ribbons in a stern but professional fashion.

"I'll try the test" said Sabrina gently.

"Alright, if you want to"

"Alex, can I barrow a pencil?" whispered Clair. Alex handed Clair a pencil when Ms. Ribbons wasn't looking. In less than five minutes Sabrina came up to the teacher's desk and handed her the test.

"Done already?" asked Ms. Ribbons surprisingly. Sabrina said nothing and just walked back to her desk. Hillary looked at Joshua.

"You can't tell me that Sabrina finished that in five minutes! Both papers of the test have at least twenty math problems on them, not including the ones Ms. Ribbons added" Hillary whispered loudly.

"She probably didn't get very many of them right" said Alex. Ms. Ribbons looked at the test papers very carefully. She looked up in with a look of surprise.

"I don't believe it, their all correct!" exclaimed Ms Ribbons.

"That's amazing!" said one of the other students. Ms. Ribbons looked at Sabrina intently. Through her entire career as a teacher, she had never met a student that had done this before.

Suddenly, it started to snow lightly outside. Clair noticed it falling.

"Is that snow...?" She walked over to the window.

"That's impossible, its way too early for snow!" she exclaimed. All the students in the classroom went over to the windows.

"It must be a freak storm or something" said Lorelei.

"Yeah, it doesn't snow at the end of May for no particular reason" Brenda agreed.

Clair glanced at Sabrina, the only student who wasn't looking out the window. Sabrina smiled at Clair and finally peered out the window. The snow came down heavier. A shivering chill ran down Clair's spine, effortlessly provoking a bizarre, uncomfortable feeling.

"Okay class, back to your seats, the bell hasn't rung yet" said Ms. Ribbons. A teacher from across the hall came into the room.

"Are you seeing this, Gladys? It's snowing!"

"Yes, I know Lotti, it's strange. Nothing like this has ever happened before, not even when I was young" Gladys replied. She was very bewildered by this event and Sabrina.

During study hall, Clair and her friends went to the library to talk and look at books.

"Hi Daphne" said Clair, as she and her friends walked through the library doors.

"Hi Clair, what brings you to the library today?" Daphne asked.

"Nothing much, I just stopped by to the look around and socialize" said Clair. Daphne Bakersfield was the school librarian and also one of Clair's friends. Daphne had babysat Clair at times when her parents went out; this was when Clair was much younger of course.

The library had an upstairs level and a downstairs level. The upper level possessed numerous nonfiction books to aid students with their homework. The lower level was comprised of fiction books available and a reference area. Clair, Alex, and Joshua were looking at books downstairs, while Hillary went upstairs to browse around. Hillary walked to the back of the bookshelf halls to a small reading area near some windows. She wanted to examine some books she had found. She was just about to sit down at one of the tables when she saw Sabrina. She was sitting at the other end of the room, near the windows. She was looking at a book as she clutched her doll in her free hand.

Hillary looked at the stack of books sitting on the table beside Sabrina. Sabrina had been reading Mathematics, Chemistry, Astronomy, and Parapsychology. Sabrina didn't notice Hillary standing at the other end of the room. Hillary was just about to say hello, when Sabrina put the book she was holding on to the stack of science books. She grabbed another book from the other end of the table. Except Sabrina didn't use her hands, she simply looked at the books and they astonishingly moved by themselves. Hillary dropped the books she was holding. Mystified by what she had just witnessed, she gasped and ran quickly down the stairs.

"Clair!" shouted Hillary as she ran toward her friend. "You've got to come upstairs with me right now!"

"What's wrong with you, stop yelling!" said Clair.

"I think I saw something weird happen upstairs. It's Sabrina. I think there is something wrong with her. I don't know, maybe I'm going crazy!" said Hillary

"What do you mean?' laughed Alex.

"Stop laughing, I'm not joking around! I thought I saw Sabrina move some books. I know this sounds impossible, but I didn't even see her touch them!" Hillary said.

"I don't understand what you're trying to say" said Joshua.

"I think I know what Hillary's saying, Josh. I thought there was something weird about Sabrina too, especially when we were watching the snow fall earlier" said Clair. "Hillary, how exactly were those books moving when you saw them move by themselves?"

"They were moving sort of awkward. Like there was no gravity holding them down" Hillary explained.

"Just as I thought. I think that Sabrina is a telekinetic, or so to speak, gifted" said Clair.

"What do you mean, telekinetic" asked Alex.

"It's actually called telekinesis, or telekinetic energy. Telekinesis is a power of the mind. It allows a person to move objects freely, without touching them. They visualize moving something in their mind and in then they move it. People, who have this power and are able to harness it, are called telekinetic" said Clair.

"Sounds cool" said Joshua.

"It can be quite dangerous at times, especially when the person gets mad. It's linked to emotions" said Clair.

Let's go upstairs and investigate the area where Sabrina was" Alex suggested.

"Good idea" said Clair. They all followed Hillary to the second floor.

"I don't see her anywhere" said Joshua.

"She was sitting right over there when I got here. She must have left" said Hillary, nervously. Clair and Alex walked over to where Sabrina had been sitting and looked at the books on the table.

"Why would she read stuff like this?" asked Alex.

"Remember when Sabrina finished that math test so quickly? She must study books like these to get smarter. Which is really not a bad idea" said Clair.

"Hillary, did you see Sabrina go anywhere?" asked Clair.

"No" answered Hillary.

"If we knew where she was, we could talk to her about this" said Joshua.

"That might not be a good idea" suggested Clair. Alex suddenly noticed a black book on the floor with a silver cat printed on the front.

"Hey, look at this book Clair" he said. Clair picked it up and opened it cautiously.

"There's a strong smell of lavender perfume on this book" said Clair.

"It looks like a diary, and it's old too" said Hillary.

"It is, property of Sabrina Eileen LaMore and Erika Hazel LaMore" said Clair as she read the writing on the first page.

"Why are there two names?" asked Joshua.

"Maybe this Erika person was the first owner of the book" said Hillary.

"Well, we should get back to class before it's over" said Alex.

They started walking out when they heard a sudden loud cracking sound. It was quick and creepy. They turned around and saw a large jagged crack through the middle of the table.

"What the hell did that?!" Alex exclaimed. Sabrina stood over by the table with her doll.

"People shouldn't take things that belong to someone else, it's impolite" said Clementine. Sabrina reached out her hand and her black book flew swiftly and perfectly into it. She then walked down a row of bookcases and was gone.

Chapter 2

Clair, Hillary, Joshua, and Alex were roaming Central Park still mesmerized at Sabrina's little show at the library. The impression weighed heavily upon them, "What should I do" pondered each adolescent. With the perpetual downfall of frigid snow, the air produced an unmerciful chill.

"Finally, a drinking fountain!" said Hillary as she sprinted over to it. They had been walking around Central Park for hours.

"It's certainly clear that you haven't been here in a while" said Joshua. Hillary stood up from the fountain.

"I know. I didn't realize how large Central Park was until now" she said. Clair and Alex sat down on a park bench beside Hillary and Joshua to rest.

"You guys, we're not going to deal with this situation if we're just wandering around town all day" said Alex.

"Well, what are we supposed to do? Wait until Sabrina wanders through the park and then *ask* her if she's telekinetic" Joshua answered.

"Let's just go home. We'll ask that man over there where the nearest subway is" Clair said. They all walked over to him briskly.

"Excuse me sir?" asked Hillary, tapping the man on the

shoulder. The man turned around, waiting for the girl to ask a question. He was tall with black hair, and was wearing a dark purple jacket.

"You all must be Clair, Hillary, Alex, and Josh" said the man. All four teens just stared at him wide-eyed. "I've been expecting you; I'm Sabrina's father, Victor."

"WHAT?!" said all four teens simultaneously.

"Please. Let me explain everything" said the man.

"Yeah, I think maybe you should" said Clair staring at the man intently. The teens all sat down on a nearby bench.

"Please listen closely to what I'm going to say" said Victor.

"Well, get on with it" said Joshua

"Okay, when Sabrina was younger, she was the happiest little girl I ever knew. My wife Erika and I treated Sabrina very well. We all lived in a large mansion in Warren, PA. It was an affluent neighborhood called Unicorn Acres. We resided there for several years. Erika and I both were always worried if Sabrina had inherited my powers when she was born. Since we didn't see any signs of this power from Sabrina, we forgot about it. Until one day, when she was eating dinner with the family: it was around Christmas time. The butler accidentally spilled wine on Sabrina while bringing it to the table. Sabrina was very upset because her new dress was ruined and it wasn't replaceable. We tried to calm her down but she wouldn't listen. Then, while Sabrina was yelling, all the dishes and glasses on the table shattered into several pieces. The bulbs and ornaments on the Christmas tree broke as well. My parents, Jeremiah and Whitney, ran out of the house asserting Sabrina was hexed and devilish witch-child. They also had previously stated: "it was just a matter of time, before Sabrina would be cursed with this corrupt, evil power."

"Erika and I were thinking, maybe Sabrina could only use this ability when she was very angry. However, Erika found Sabrina twisting silverware, splintering the wooden cupboards and the sink faucet, well, it simply exploded. All of this destruction was caused by a run-of-the-mill headache. Erika became afraid of Sabrina, afraid that she might hurt her, or worse, someone else. Sabrina was a very talented girl. She learned ventriloquism and became a Ventriloquist. I even bought her a doll, which she named Clementine. She began to constantly use it, she used it almost as if it were alive. A wooden version of herself. The doll became her voice. Sometimes I would ask Sabrina "how are you feeling?" or "what would you like the cook to make for dinner?" She would never answer, not Sabrina. The doll would talk for her saying: "Sabrina doesn't want to talk now, ask again later" or "Sabrina wants her favorite ice cream, and nothing else." The doll was really beginning to disturb me, but I let Sabrina use it, because she was comfortable using it. Sabrina was also a good singer by the time she was thirteen. Unfortunately, she only sang alone in her room.

She loved to listen to music from the 50's through the 80's. Sometimes you could hear her records playing from her room. They echoed through the halls of the house. I remember one time I could hear the song "Mr. Sandman" playing in the distance. That was a popular song in the mid 50's. Even though we thought Sabrina was happy, she really wasn't. Due to lack of happiness and sheer boredom, she accepted her gift; she practiced using her powers. These talents were developed. She used them more and more, until they became much stronger and more frightening.

"What were her limits?" This question boggled my mind and relentlessly fueled my anxieties.

Over time, Sabrina developed some new powers. She discovered that she could fabricate psycho illusions. She could actually control how others view reality, creating a unique illusion. Imagine, a single thought of an eighteen year old girl and "wham," the invention of you own personal fantasy. Worse yet, the invasion of your worst fear. She could control weather, teleport from one place to another, and heat up anything until it burst into flames. A type of pyrokinesis, except not quite as strong. Above all, her strongest ability was telekinesis; the ability to move objects with one's mind. Sabrina was naturally, nearly invincible.

After several somewhat public displays of Sabrina's powers, her reputation began to proceed her. I noticed several of our acquaintances conveniently and quickly moving out from our neighborhood. I guess they realized who exactly lived next door. Others, of course stayed, believing the rumors had to be fantastic lies. Erika couldn't take it anymore. She threatened to murder Sabrina and tried to shoot her in a frantic, final solution to the "Sabrina situation." She managed to find one of my shotguns, although I thought I had hidden them rather well.

"Why would Sabrina do all of this in the first place?" asked Hillary.

"I don't know, she had everything she wanted due to our prosperity. Possibly, it was natural for Sabrina to experiment with her powers. It must have crossed her mind that she could do whatever she pleased and no one could possibly stop her. Another possible reason was, she was so intelligent that her brain developed more and more. Often when an individual resorts to employing pure logic to find solutions to their problems, there is a lack of compassion. Example, a self-proclaimed, logically driven, dictator, Mr. Adolph Hitler. He employed several "logical" solutions to his country's problems. Sabrina's powers could have produced some pretty logical but radical solutions to her many problems. Once she realized that logic wasn't the answer, she must have decided to be more emotional. The problem with this is, once someone or something upsets Sabrina, an emotional response could only be spiteful. With her abilities came too much power and responsibility. Simply being mad resulted in either a logical solution of getting rid of the problem or reacting with an emotional response to people's fears. Either way, she could not win."

Victor continued on with the story. "When Erika was practically shooting everything it the house, going psychotic and trying to kill Sabrina. Sabrina ran into the kitchen and stood at one corner, looked at the ceiling, and made it collapse onto Erika. Erika had supposedly died immediately. I ran over to Sabrina, getting ready to slam her into the wall, hopefully beating some sense into her head. My response was purely emotional; it never crossed my mind that I was no match for her. Even with my own power. She was simply stronger than me."

Clair put her hands over her mouth in a gasp. "Sabrina threw me against the wall instead and then simply teleported away. I haven't seen her since then, until today. I'm now having the foremost investigators searching for Erika's body. We haven't found it yet, but we know she isn't at the house anymore" said Victor.

Clair, Hillary, Josh, and Alex were just sitting there wishing they were somewhere else doing something different at the moment.

"Sabrina must be in distress, mentally" said Hillary.

"Yeah, she's obviously upset about something" added Alex. Clair quickly spotted two people standing behind a tree, tying to hide.

"Who's over there?" Clair asked, walking over to the tree. The two people came out of hiding.

"We heard the whole thing" said Gloria.

"What are you two doing here?" asked Joshua. Gloria and Harlene had been passing by when Victor told the story.

"Who are these two?" Victor asked.

"These two are Gloria Johnson and Harlene Coleman" said Clair, pointing o both of them.

"Hi Victor, call me Harley" said Harlene.

"Yeah...hi, we were wondering if we could help you track down Sabrina?" asked Gloria.

"You mean that you two are actually going to help somebody?" asked Clair, being sardonic.

"We heard what Sabrina is really like, and a lot of people are in danger around here, so *we'll all just have to get along*" said Harlene.

"Are you going to tell Brenda and Lorelei about this too?" Clair asked.

"No, it's better if they don't know" said Gloria.

"Well, its bad enough that you two know" said Hillary.

"You're going to have to keep this a secret, do you understand me?" Clair protested as she got up in Harlene's face.

"Okay, okay we will. Jeez, someone needs a pill" Harlene answered referring to Clair.

"I will be back later to talk with you all" said Victor. He then teleported away, leaving all six teenagers stuck with the situation.

"What are we supposed to do now, Harley?!" Gloria asked roughly.

"I don't know I'm not the question queen!" snapped Harlene.

"We all have a fieldtrip to Coney Island on Monday. We'll look for Sabrina there" said Clair.

"Clair, there are too many people there, what if she does something drastic?!" asked Hillary.

"If worst come to worst, we're just going to have to try and stop her" said Alex.

"Agreed" said Gloria and Harlene. All six teens then went home to wait for Monday to come.

Chapter 3

Clair quickly finished her dinner and started to call Alex on the phone to see if he was ready to go to the movie theater. It was Sunday night and Alex and Joshua wanted to go see a movie with Clair and Hillary to keep their minds of the Sabrina situation.

"Harley and Gloria are already waiting for us at the theater" said Alex, as Clair got into his convertible. Hillary and Joshua were in the back seat.

"I'll see you later mom" said Clair. Clair's mother waved bye to them as Alex drove off. It had stopped snowing and it wasn't cold anymore, so Alex had the top down on his convertible to enjoy the night zephyr.

"It's eerie how it stopped snowing" said Hillary.

"I know, now it's almost like it never happened" said Joshua. Alex turned on the car radio to listen to some music when suddenly a newsflash cam on.

"This is television reporter Mary Walker reporting from Manhattan Area High School. Friday, around four in the afternoon, a tragic accident killed two women. The school's library's ceiling mysteriously collapsed, killing these two victims;

Gladys Ribbons and Daphne Bakersfield. The police have checked the area several times, but there aren't any clues on why the ceiling collapsed. Mr. Edmund and Rosa Bakersfield have announced that they are suing Manhattan Area High for defective construction of the roof. The mayor has closed the school until this mystery is resolved. This has been a news report from Mary Walker. I'll follow up on this report at the ten o'clock news tonight." The radio went back to its original broadcast.

Clair put her hands over mouth and gasped.

"Oh my god!" shouted Hillary. Alex quickly pulled off to the side of the curb and shut off the radio. Clair threw her arms around Alex and cried. "I can't believe something like this would happen!" said Hillary. Joshua looked at Alex.

"How does a ceiling just collapse for no reason?" he asked.

"There has to be an explanation for it" said Alex. Clair instantly remembered something.

"Wait a minute, Sabrina was at the library earlier that day" she said.

"She could be the cause of all this" explained Hillary. Alex pulled back into traffic and headed for the movie theater. As he parked the car, Gloria and Harlene ran over to them.

"Did you hear what happened at the school?!" shouted Harlene. Clair wiped tears from her eyes.

"Yes" she said. "We heard it on the radio just before we got here."

"I'll bet Sabrina did it" Gloria said.

"We figured that too" said Hillary.

"Well, we better get in there, the movie is just about to start. It will keep our minds off what happened" Harlene implied.

They all walked into the theater's main doors. They walked into a large red walled hallway that had many seats in the front.

"Our seats are right above us in the upper balcony" said Harlene.

"Harley, I don't think I'm going to be able to go up there" said Hillary.

"Why not?' Harlene asked vindictively.

"Hillary's afraid of heights" said Clair.

"Well, you have to, they are the only seats left" said Harlene as she started up the staircase.

"Don't worry, I'll sit right beside you" said Joshua affectionately. Hillary agreed and they went up to the balcony with a cluster of other people.

"We're sitting in the middle of the front row" said Harlene.

They walked alongside a gold balustrade along the edge of the balcony until they came to their seats and sat down.

"How long is the movie supposed to be?' Hillary asked.

"I don't remember, just relax, you'll be fine when the movie starts" said Joshua as he put his arm around Hillary. Clair got up from her seat.

"I'll be right back" she said.

"Where are you going?" Alex asked.

"Just to the restroom" answered Clair.

About five minutes later when Clair came out of the bathroom, she saw Sabrina open the front doors of the theater harshly and walk in with an emotionless look across her face. Sabrina saw Clair and walked toward her.

"Hi Clair, would you like to play?" asked Sabrina's doll pleasantly but ominously.

"Stay away from me!" Clair yelled as she ran up the stairs.

"Childish fool" said Sabrina emphatically with a dry, sinister articulation.

"Alex, Sabrina's in the theater!" Clair whispered dreadfully.

"What are you talking about?' asked Harlene bluntly.

"She's in here, I saw her downstairs!" said Clair. Alex looked down at the movie screen. Sabrina was standing in the middle of the picture for attention.

"Clair isn't lying, there she is!" Alex said pointing. Other people pointed and talked, wondering why she was there. The movie stopped and the lights came on. A guard walked toward Sabrina frantically.

"What are you doing over there young lady?' questioned the guard with a loud voice. Sabrina spoke.

"This movie is stealing my show" she said gloomily. Then Sabrina stared at the guard firmly and he burst into flames. The guard flew into frenzy, screeching the worst high pitched, offensive sound. The resonance of this noise left people standing horrified, mouths agape and absolutely mortified at what they just witnessed. Then the people in the audience began panicking, they scrambled around in pandemonium, a frantic plea for their lives. The cries were deafening, howls, shrieks, and finally the most miserable, inconceivable scene of utter chaos and destruction followed. The flames engulfed everyone and everything, the entire structure was consumed.

"Let's get out of here before we all die!" clamored Gloria. Sabrina glanced at the balcony quickly. Several cracks fissured through it and broke it apart. Gloria fell to her death screaming all the way down. The balcony only fell half way, dangling like a loose tooth. Clair fell, but grabbed the railing and was hanging on to it for dear life. Harlene and Alex gradually made their way down to the edge of the balcony, grabbed Clair's hand and pulled her up to safety. The balcony finally broke off and fell into the inferno below. Clair and her friends ran toward the theater doors, but before they could escape, Sabrina closed and locked them.

They all turned around and looked at Sabrina standing in the flames. The incandescent glow surrounded her, yet it was apparent that she controlled this grotesque scene. Nothing would harm her, she alone was immune.

"So now, it is time to play" said Sabrina languidly but ghastly. Sabrina put her doll down on the floor. The doll was holding a large cerulean blue ball. Sabrina then stared at Hillary. The doll became colossal. It grew up to the ceiling.

"Let's play catch Hillary" said Clementine as she rolled the enormous ball toward the teens. The ball voraciously and swiftly advanced towards them gaining momentum every second.

"Run!" shouted Joshua. Suddenly Victor emerged out of nowhere. He grabbed the teens and teleported them and himself out of the theater to safety. The ball rolled into the doors, crushing them on impact. Sabrina was furious.

"He's back again" she told herself. Her doll returned back to its normal size and she teleported away just as several fire trucks arrived at the scene.

Victor and the teenagers arrived at Central Park moments later.

"I ought to slam you right now!" yelled Alex angrily, as he raised his fist toward Victor. Joshua held him back.

"Just calm down!" said Victor.

"Where in the hell were you when all those people died! Gloria is dead because of you!" Harlene yelled.

"I know that you're all angry with me, but it wasn't my fault that Gloria and those people died. It was Sabrina's fault" said Victor.

"It doesn't matter whose fault it was! You still could have come earlier and helped those people! You can't tell me that you didn't know Sabrina was at the theater, otherwise you wouldn't have come at all!" said Clair. Victor was dumbfounded. "I'm sorry for yelling Victor, but you've got to help too. We're all in this together" said Clair calmly.

"Don't mind Harlene, she's just upset like the rest of us" said Hillary.

"You kids should all go home for the rest of the day. I will see you tomorrow. Remember to be prepared for Sabrina's actions. I'm sorry, but you're all a part of this now according to Sabrina. For some reason she has taken a particular liking in tormenting you all" said Victor. He teleported again and the teens went home.

Chapter 4

The next morning, Alex picked up his friends with his car and headed for Coney Island. All of the other students were there, riding the rides. Alex parked the convertible, put up the windows and the top, and locked the doors.

"We better not split up, let's just stay together" suggested Hillary.

"When we ride the rides we'll have fun, but also watch for Sabrina or anything odd" said Clair.

"What ride do you guys want to go on first?" Harlene asked. Clair looked at the fast moving ride alongside her.

"How about this one, Harley?"

"Yeah, the Crazy Dance, I haven't been on that ride for a while"

"Good idea, I want to start the day off with something fast anyway" said Alex.

They waited in line until it was their turn. The teenagers gathered into one of the subdivided sections of seats, sociably grouped together. Alex and Clair sat in one seat, Hillary and Joshua sat together in another. Harlene sat alone, but she sat in the same party of seats with the others.

"I'm surprised that our parents even let us outside today after what happened last night" said Harlene.

"I know, but let's just try not to think about it" said Hillary. The ride started up with a guttural tone and began to move. The main platform, slightly tilted, spun around in a large circle. Each subsection of seats, twisted the group in smaller circles, at a faster velocity. The ride managed to make one, double dizzy and often sick.

"Are you having fun yet?!" yelled Alex as he hugged Clair.

"Yeah, you bet I am!" replied Clair happily. They were all in a better mood for the time being.

When the Crazy Dance stopped, the teens got off. They quickly went on to the next ride; they chose the Tilt-a-Whirl. All of them sat in the same seat and laughed as the ride revolved them around. After they got off the ride, the teens went to some nearby eating tables. They got some cola to drink and sat down. Clair suddenly noticed Sabrina standing over by a ride called The Scrambler; she delighted in watching go around and around.

"It figures she would be here" said Clair obviously distressed and disappointed.

"Do you think she knows we're here?" asked Hillary. Clair just slurped her pop and disregarded the succession of images that readily bustled through her mind.

"It doesn't look it, but she might" answered Harlene.

"Let's stay out of her sight, just in case she does know" said Joshua. Sabrina then walked away from The Scrambler and went over to the Wave Swinger. She gazed at it and then went over to the Music Express. Her reaction was the same, mindless yet contented stare.

"What's she doing" asked Hillary.

"It looks like she's just watching all the rides" said Harlene.

"That's not all she's doing, she's studying all of the rides as well. She's seeing how they work and move!" said Clair dramatically.

"She might be getting ready to attack everybody!" exclaimed Hillary.

"We don't really know that for sure, she could just be looking at them like Harley said" replied Joshua. Sabrina then looked at the Wonder Wheel, the Crazy Dance, and the Round Up. An hour had gone by and Sabrina had looked at ever ride in the park. Nevertheless, nothing dreadful had happened. She was now sitting on bench with her doll, eating an ice cream cone.

"This is so boring, why can't Victor do this?!" shouted Hillary.

"You're telling me!" said Alex with a sharp tone. A guard came walking over.

"Why are you kids just sitting around? You should be having fun" said the guard.

"We just ate a whole lot of junk food. We're resting before we go on any more rides" answered Harlene quickly.

"Okay, well have a nice day" waved the guard.

"Smart thinking" said Clair.

Alex looked over at the bench where Sabrina had been sitting, except she wasn't there.

"Clair, where's Sabrina!" he yelled.

"What, I don't know" she answered.

"She was just there" said Joshua.

"Well, where is she?" asked Harlene.

"She's just…gone!" said Alex.

"We have to find her now!" yelled Clair. They all looked around, but they couldn't find her.

"We'll never find her, it's just too crowded!" shouted Hillary.

"Oh come on Hillary, there is only so many places she could be!" said Harlene looking around in all directions.

"She's probably on one of the rides, or she's hiding from us" said Joshua.

"Isn't there a control booth or breaker box that controls the main electrical system of the rides?" asked Hillary.

"Good thinking Hillary. We'll shut down all the rides, and see if Sabrina gets off any of them" suggested Clair.

"How are we supposed to sneak past security?' asked Harlene.

"We'll have to distract them" said Clair. The breaker boxes were left unattended at the moment, so the teens went over to them and started pulling down all the switches.

Harlene saw all the rides sluggishly come to a halt. Groups of teenagers and agitated people were shouting and wondering why the rides stopped. Ride operators were checking the rides and control boxes.

"Come on, we better scram before someone sees us here" said Alex. They looked for Sabrina at every ride, but she wasn't to be found. Harlene slammed the side of a concession stand.

"This is driving me crazy, and I need a cigarette!" she demanded.

"Where in the hell is she anyway?!" Alex asked. Hillary looked around and then eerily looked up.

"She's up there, on the Sky Ride" she said pointing. Sabrina vaulted into the air with a flip and landed on the ground with ease.

"Whoa" said Alex in surprise.

"So, you think it's fun to test Sabrina's patience" Clementine said. All the lights on the rides flickered on and off with a clicking, buzzing sound. Without warning, people began to fly through the air. Men, women and children, everyone began smoking and bursting into flames.

"Stop it now Sabrina your killing everybody!" yelled Harlene. Sabrina then snapped the cable wires on the Sky Ride and people fell to the ground screaming. Through the smoke and stench of burning hair and clothes, everyone began running to the parking lot in frenzy.

"So…do you have a problem with that…Harley" Clementine said.

Lots of people got away, but some were either dead or stuck on the rides. Lorelei and Brenda ran over to Clair.

"What's going on?" asked Lorelei.

"Is Sabrina even human?" asked Brenda.

"Get out of here while you're still alive!" said Clair.

"We'll handle this" said Harlene. Lorelei and Brenda started dashing for the parking lot.

"So now, it is time to play" Sabrina said again. Brenda was suddenly thrown through the air and landed on a concession stand with glass and metal shooting through her body. Her blood sprayed everywhere. Sabrina picked up the cable wire from the Sky Ride and it was walloped through Lorelei, cutting her in two clean-cut pieces. Clair and her friends started running for their lives.

"Oh no you don't, I'm not finished with you five yet!" yelled Sabrina. She lifted Clair, Harlene, Joshua, and Alex off the ground and placed them in some vacant seats on The Scrambler; she powerfully locked the bars overlapping the seats.

"Get us out of here! Alex shouted.

"Just relax, rides were meant to be fun" said Sabrina in a depraved voice. Hillary was running as fast as she could try to get away from the situation. Sabrina grabbed her as well and put her on the Round Up.

"Leave me alone!" Hillary shrieked. Sabrina started up the ride.

"Round and round you go, where you'll stop, nobody knows" said Clementine playfully. The ride started to go sideways and gain acceleration. Sabrina turned around to attend to the screaming people on the Wonder Wheel.

"Let us down!" The people were stranded in the seats, at Sabrina's mercy. Sabrina walked up to the large Ferris Wheel.

"I'll let you down" she spoke shrewdly. Clair heard a loud "crack" and was drown to the Wonder Wheel. To her amazement, the hub ruptured and the large wheel came booming down to the ground. Passengers bounced out with immense force and were propelled through every obstacle in their path.

"Oh my god!" she exclaimed. Unexpectedly, every ride in the park started. First the Wave swinger, then The Whip, the Paratrooper, and so on. The Scrambler started as well.

"Let's go for a little ride" said Clementine.

"How do we get off this thing?!" Harlene yelled.

"We can't, it's moving too fast!" answered Clair.

They were all about to lose hope and accept their demise. Out of nowhere appeared Lynda Lark from behind a concession stand. She quickly shut off The Scrambler. After the ride ceased, they all ran towards the Round Up to help Hillary. Alex stopped the ride and Clair ran onto the walk area. Hillary laid there with her eyes closed.

"Hillary wake up, please don't be dead!" shouted Clair. Clair gently pulled Hillary from her seat and shook her with just enough exertion to wake her.

"Hillary's not dead, she's just unconscious" said Alex.

"Come on, we have to get out of here" Lynda said. Alex and Joshua both carried Hillary. Sabrina suddenly appeared in front of them. Without regard to Sabrina's capabilities, Lynda screamed angrily; "Get out of the way!" Sabrina's eyes gleamed with a crimson-like glow as she stared firmly into Lynda's eyes. Suddenly, Lynda began screaming uncontrollably and running around in circles as if something horrific was chasing her.

"What's wrong with her?" asked Joshua.

"Lynda must have seen something that really wasn't there, like a psycho illusion" said Clair. Lynda ran away from Sabrina as fast as she could. Hillary woke up and was glad to see her friends. All five teens ran toward the parking lot. Alex quickly opened the car doors. Sabrina looked at the Wave Swinger and all the hanging seats snapped off and flew toward Alex's convertible, like a row of darting eagles closing in on a prey.

"Get in now!" yelled Alex. The seats hit the convertibles side, and hood. The car had some major dents, but could still move. Sabrina angrily gritted her teeth and teleported to the parking lot. Alex stomped on the gas pedal. Sabrina powerfully tore off the folding roof of the convertible. Hillary screamed. Realizing Alex was driving away from her, Sabrina got into one of the cars nearest to her, a Ford Thunderbird.

Chapter 5

Sabrina and Alex were soon weaving in and out of traffic, playing a deadly game of cat and mouse.

"Do you think we can out run her" asked Harlene.

"I don't know she's gaining on us" said Alex. Sabrina threw cars out of her way as she sped down the street. Alex tried to escape from Sabrina, but a Volvo station wagon was in the way. Sabrina removed her hands from the wheel and began driving the Thunderbird with her power. Concentrating on the teenager's vehicle, she peered through her windshield and readied a stumbling block to slow them down. She blew out the Volvo's left front tire and it spun sidelong to the right, quickly blocking the group's path. Alex abruptly veered onto the sideway. Sparks flew from the jolting concussion with the curb and barely missed colliding into the Volvo. Traffic that was behind Alex, clobbered into the Volvo and bulldozed it down the street. People scurried out of Alex's way as he flew down the sidewalk without regard or reverence to anything or anyone.

"Alex this dangerous, get us off the sidewalk!" yelled Harlene.

"I'm trying to, just shut up!" he answered. Sabrina laughed and sadistically relished the immediate jeopardy she had exacted on the group of teens.

The finally came to the ending of the block and Alex quickly darted off the sidewalk with a thunderous crash.

"When is going to give up?" asked Hillary

"She probably won't!" Clair answered. Alex quickly pulled along side Sabrina and tried to run her off the road. A parked car was just pulling out into traffic as Alex and Sabrina drove right toward it. Sabrina got away by tuning onto a side street, ramming a little Geo Metro right off the road. Alex swerved and he took off the other car's left side door mirror. Hillary screamed as the shattered mirror flew right between Joshua's and Harlene's heads.

Alex turned the car down the side street and started after Sabrina. Since Sabrina was busy looking through the back window of the Thunderbird, she didn't notice another car heading right toward her. She laughed at them again and turned around to grab the steering wheel. Sabrina saw the approaching car and screamed. She quickly tried to avoid it, but she drove right over the other car and soared through the air sideways. When the Thunderbird hit the ground, it crashed with tremendous force and rolled down the street. The sound was deafening. The clamorous tension of strained metal and glass was inconceivable, as the car rolled over and over again. Alex instantaneously stomped on his breaks. The five teens got out of the car and bolted toward the demolished Thunderbird. Sabrina crawled out of the window with her doll, and had a massive bleeding gash across her forehead. Sabrina saw the teens and fervently gestured "away with you!" The five teens flew through the air and were hurled to the ground. Alex sat up.

"I really don't think she likes us" he said helping up his friends.

Clair looked at Sabrina coming toward them. Her eyes were glowing bright scarlet, she almost didn't look human. A restaurant that was behind the teens opened its doors and they were catapulted inside. Sabrina then slammed the doors shut and they were firmly locked.

"Where are we?" asked Hillary.

"We're in The Little Classic Café. My mom and I come here to eat once in a while. It's designed to look like a restaurant for the 50's" said Joshua.

"We can't get out, she's locked us in here" said Harlene as she pulled on the door. Alex looked at the chairs at the dining tables.

"We can't even use the chairs to break the windows, they're bolted to the floor" he said. Suddenly the jukebox that was sitting in a corner started playing "Sh-Boom" by The Crew Cuts. Sabrina walked away and left them there. Behind her was a scene of mayhem and utter destruction.

"We're going to have to figure out how to get out of here and stop her soon!" Clair said. The teens all sat down to think and rest, while the jukebox played.

"Well, this is the first time, but, I really don't know what to do" said Clair. She was sitting in one of the table's booths, distastefully folding her arms. Alex walked over to her and sat alongside her. The jukebox stated playing the "Locomotion" by Little Eva. Harlene got up and went over to the jukebox.

"There has to be a way to shut this thing up! Isn't there a button…or a switch?" she asked. Joshua went over and started pulling the jukebox out of the corner.

"What are you doing?" Harlene asked.

"Help me pull it out, we have to take the plug out of the wall" said Joshua. They dragged it out and Harlene snatched the plug. The jukebox still played steadily.

44

"Well that figures!" said Hillary rolling her eyes.

"Oh great, now I'm stuck in here with a possessed musical box!" yelled Harlene. She raised her leg slammed the front of the jukebox with a kick. The record went off balance and the needle went into a brief crackling sound. The music died.

"Harley, just let it go, I'll buy you a punching bag for Christmas" said Alex.

Clair looked out the window again. A news van drove up near Sabrina. A woman and a man with a video camera came out.

"Hey, isn't that TV reporter Mary Walker?' Clair asked.

"Yeah, she must be trying to get Sabrina on camera" said Joshua.

"She has to get away from her, she has no idea who she's dealing with!" yelled Hillary. Sabrina stood in the middle of the street with her eyes closed. The sky got dark and stormy. The camera man saw what was happening. He got into the van and drove off with the tires squealing. Sabrina turned around and saw Mary standing there looking at her with interest.

"Come on, we have to get out and save her!" shouted Clair. She ran to the back of the café and found a rear exit. Alex followed behind and gently pushed Clair aside to break open the door after several kicks. The gang of teens ran out to the front of the café, and when they got there, Sabrina was staring into the gloomy sky. A concentrated expression ran across her vacuous face, and with a crack, a lightning bolt exploded out of the sky. Mary was dead instantly. Her deceased, smoldering body lay on the ground, charred and putrid with the stink of burnt hair and flesh. Sabrina looked at the teens.

"How the hell did you get out?" she asked.

"You should have known by now that you can't keep us away!" said Clair. Sabrina, appalled, peered at Clair for a moment.

She then turned away from her, dismissing Clair's persistence. Hillary suddenly had an idea. She ran over to the police cars that had previously swarmed the area. The officers were busy shooting at Sabrina, but the bullets were soaring around her.

"Stop shooting at *her*, aim for the doll!" Hillary yelled. The officer aimed right for Sabrina's doll and shot it. The doll's porcelain clay head shattered into several pieces.

"NO!" Sabrina shouted.

"Excellent thinking Hillary, that's the only way to get to Sabrina!" said Clair. Sabrina stood over her doll lying on the roadway, staring at it woefully. Her eyes filled with warm tears. She picked up the broken pieces and Clementine's body.

Harlene looked over at Sabrina.

"Um, Clair, I don't think that was a good idea" she said tapping Clair's shoulder. The teens all looked at Sabrina. She was infuriated. Her eyes were fixed on them.

"Your bones will shatter for this!" she yelled defiantly. Her rage began to build rapidly. Then, it happened. Her rage exploded. As if a volcanic blast erupted underground, the roadway fissured with large cracks and sent a gigantic wall of large asphalt fragments passing Sabrina with ease. The ground tore up fiendishly, heading straight for the teens and officers. Joshua saw a car parked in an alley between the café and another large building.

"Quick, get in that car!" he yelled. They all scrambled to the car and got in. The wall of jagged pieces flew past. A dust fog surrounded the car and the teens couldn't see outside.

Soon, everything was quiet. Alex opened the door and immediately noticed a change in temperature. They all came out and realized they weren't even in the same city anymore.

"Clair, where are we?" Harlene asked. They all looked around in amazement.

"We're in Tokyo, Japan!" Clair answered.

"How do you know that?" asked Joshua.

"Because...we're on top of the famous Tokyo Tower!" said Clair. Hillary started shaking and fell to the floor.

"This is way too high up!" she exclaimed.

Clair went over beside Hillary to help her calm down.

"How are we supposed to get home?!" asked Harlene as she looked out over the deck.

"Sabrina put us here on purpose!" yelled Hillary. Alex looked around the deck, no one else was around.

"It must be late at night over here, everyone's at home" he said.

"The doors are locked too" said Joshua.

Sabrina then appeared in front of them. She walked calmly over to the railing on the deck and looked out at the city.

"Isn't Tokyo gorgeous at night, I've always wanted to come here" she said softly.

"Why are you acting so nice all of a sudden?!" asked Harlene rudely.

"Shh, be quiet, she having a mood swing, we don't want to upset her" said Clair. Clair walked over. Sabrina looked forlorn and had tears flowing down her face.

"Are you alright, Sabrina?' asked Clair in a concerned way.

"No...I'm not, and I probably never will be!" she cried.

"Sabrina, has something been bothering you all this time?" Clair asked.

"It's just...the way my life is...never mind, you probably don't understand anyway, just like everyone else" Sabrina spoke.

"If you tell me what the matter is, I can try to understand" said Clair.

"I really miss my mom; I didn't mean to do what I did. Haven't you ever felt so alone, stressed and depressed; you felt as though there was no way out? And, everyone is always mean to you for no reason at all, just because...I'm different. That's how I feel all the time. Sometimes it's fun to have powers, but look at what I've done with my life. I almost killed you and your friends; I've killed so many other people! "I'm so very, very tired of living!" Sabrina yelled.

"Don't say that about yourself! You're a very special person to have what you have! We all make mistakes Sabrina. In your case you made many *big* mistakes, but only *you* can change your life" said Clair.

"Clair...just leave me alone!" Sabrina shouted. She teleported everyone back to New York.

Clair realized that her and her friends were now on the top of the Empire State Building. Sabrina was above, floating in the dark sky. Lightning was striking all around.

"Sabrina, stop this now!" yelled Harlene.

"Sabrina, I know your upset, but you can't hurt everyone else just because you're angry!" shouted Clair. The Empire State Building started to shake.

"Oh my god, we're going to die!" yelled Hillary. Sabrina turned her attention to teens. For a brief moment, Clair could see the hurt in Sabrina's eyes. A lightning bolt suddenly shot out of the sky and hit Sabrina. She fell down to the ground out of sight.

"SABRINA!" Clair called out. The weather soon died down as the teens reached the city streets. When they got there, Sabrina was being put into a black bag and was on her way to the city morgue.

"We could have saved her!" Clair sobbed as she hugged Alex tensely.

Clean up soon began in the city. People were roaming about the city for days, amazed at the destruction. Brenda's, Lorelei's, and Gloria's parents all had funerals for their children, although, the murdered teenagers had to be placed in closed caskets. As for Lynda Lark, she'd now spend her time in a psychiatric hospital, having hallucinations of giant spiders trying to bite her head off. Meanwhile, at the city morgue, Sabrina woke up. She solemnly climbed off the observation table and looked about the room. She saw Clementine sitting beside her on a chair. With an eerie smile, she grabbed her and teleported away.

Part 2

Sabrina's Reprisal

Chapter 6

Snow was falling all over Manhattan. The kind of heavy wet flakes that causes no school for a week. Clair watched it fall from 14 stories up. She worked for a very successful company in New York City and was Vice President. The company was called Lost Hearts. It specialized on aiding people with psychological, social, or emotional problems. The agency basically helped anyone who was depressed for any reason. Clair's personal secretary came into the office.

"Wow, it's really coming down out there isn't it. I do love snow, it makes the world a little bit magical" said Ann. Ann Jenner has been Clair secretary for two years now, and they have become good friends.

"Ann, have you heard from Alex yet? Shouldn't he be out of work by now?" asked Clair impatiently.

"No not yet Miss Nelson. You know he's fine though, a little powder snow hasn't stopped him from calling before" said Ann.

"Yeah, I guess you're right. Ann, you know you can call me Clair. We've been friends for a while now" said Clair.

"I know I'm just being courteous" answered Ann. Clair noticed a yellow file folder, Ann was holding.

"What's that Ann? Something for me?" Clair asked.

"Oh, yes, I forgot. I received this from a family called LaMore" said Ann handing Clair the folder. Clair sank in her chair.

"LaMore?" she asked prudently.

"Yeah, some delivery guy said it came from Warren, PA" answered Ann.

Clair dropped the folder and stared out the window blankly.

"Are you okay, you look like you've seen a ghost, Clair" said Ann.

"I'm fine!" said Clair quickly. Ann jumped back.

"Are you sure?" she asked.

"Yes! Yes, I am, sorry about the outburst. I just haven't heard that name in six years" said Clair.

"Well, alright. I'll bring you some coffee" said Ann.

"Yeah, thanks" said Clair.

After Ann left the room, Clair was alone. She opened the folder cautiously.

"What's this about anyway" she said to herself. Inside was a letter that said:

Dear Miss Clair Nelson,

My name is Dmitri Vallenway. I'm the butler of the LaMore's in Warren, Pennsylvania. I have been asked to invite you to a stay at LaMore Manor, where some old information and experiences will be reunited. You will be staying with the following people, Mr. Joshua Deller, Miss Hillary Dunn, and Miss Harlene Coleman. We also would appreciate your fiancé, Alexander Sanderson to come along too. There are some new people you'll meet here as well. Hope to see you here by Friday December 10th.

Sincerely,

Dmitri Vallenway and the LaMore family

Clair closed the folder and called for Ann.

"Yes, Clair?" said Ann.

"Could you cover for me for a while, I have to leave on a trip. A business trip." said Clair.

"Sorry, no. I'm leaving tomorrow for Lansing Michigan to see relatives" said Ann.

"No problem, I'll just call Eartha then" said Clair.

"Eartha Phamm? She's in San Diego for two weeks" said Ann.

"Well, who else is there?" asked Clair.

"Basically no one other than Octavia Rain and Lawrence is busy being the boss" said Ann.

"Okay" said Clair, reaching for her phone.

"It's just for a couple of weeks, Octavia. I'll be back soon" said Clair.

"Well, alright. I'll cover for you, but don't be gone forever" said Octavia sternly. Clair hung up.

"Have a good trip, Clair" said Ann.

The next day, Clair and Alex caught a bus to Warren County, PA. Clair was very straight forward with her fiancé on why they were leaving New York.

"Are you sure about this, Clair? Remember, Sabrina was reported missing and possibly alive the day after she was struck by lightning" said Alex.

"I know, but it would be fascinating to see her home, don't you think?" asked Clair.

"Well, I guess so" said Alex. Deep down, Alex was afraid of going to LaMore Manor, and Clair wouldn't admit she was even more fearful. Although, for some reason, she felt drawn to go there. It was the same kind of ominous feeling that she experienced when Sabrina gave her that menacing look on the day they met.

Chapter 7

Soon after the long bus ride to Warren, Clair and Alex found a large white limousine waiting for them at the bus station. A tall man in a butler's suit and dark hair came out of the limo quickly and spoke with a British accent.

"Good afternoon. I'm Dmitri, I will be taking you to LaMore Manor" he said.

"Thank you Mr. Vallenway" said Clair cordially.

The limousine took them to a large mansion that was hidden behind thick evergreen tree down a long driveway. It was built in a gothic design and had a dejected look. It was indeed colossal, almost six stories of house. It wasn't just a mansion, it was a castle. Across the top of the doorway read LaMore Manor 1833. Most windows were made with elegance and stained glass. Dmitri stopped the car and opened Clair's door.

"Welcome to LaMore Manor madam" he said.

They all walked inside and they saw their old friends.

"Alex! Clair! I can't believe it's you!" said Hillary. Clair hugged her friend and then saw Harlene standing behind.

"Hi Harley!" said Clair, and hugged her as well.

"It's nice to see you again too Clair. I missed you" said Harlene.

"We're all together again" said Joshua.

Suddenly two women and a girl that was about nineteen came into the large front hall.

"Hello everyone, and welcome. "I'm Meredith LaMore and this is Gabriella LaMore and her daughter Eleanor" said Meredith.

"Hello" said Gabriella. Eleanor didn't speak. Victor came in as well.

"I trust your journeys were gratifying?" he asked.

"Yes, Victor, but why are we all here?" Harlene asked.

"Well, Harley, because my daughter is still alive, and so is my wife. Everyone, this is Erika" said Victor. A tall woman with chestnut brown hair came in serenely. She was wearing a shimmering dark blue dress that matched her blue eyes and showed her good figure.

"Erika? I thought you were dead" said Alex.

"So did I" said Hillary.

"After Sabrina collapsed the ceiling on me, I was terrified. I just had to get far away from her and the whole situation. I crawled out from the rubble, and ran as fast as I could, far from everything and everyone. So, I basically disappeared for a while. I realized that I made a huge mistake, tying to get rid of my daughter. Ironically, I ended up doing just that. I scared her off. I went to find her; I wanted so badly to apologize for my actions. The more I looked, the more I realized, she was simply non-existent" said Erika.

"Erika came back months later and stayed with me. My sister, Gabriella and her daughter Eleanor came to live with us later" said Victor.

"As well as my sister, Meredith" said Erika.

"Why did you stay away so long though?" asked Clair.

"Because I wasn't going to stop looking for her" said Erika.

"But, you did anyhow" Harlene added.

"Yes" Erika answered solemnly.

"Well, I suppose we should show you all to your rooms now. Feel free to roam about the house, you may find some interesting rooms here" said Victor.

Suddenly a corpulent looking maid with dark red hair came into the room. She was wearing a French maid's outfit. She looked about forty years of age and spoke with a Russian accent.

"Dinner will be ready by 7:00. Tonight's recipe is Duck Alaronz, please dress for the occasion" she announced presently.

"Thank you, Rosario" Gabriella called.

"Please follow me to the staircase in the east wing" said Dmitri. As they all followed, they passed the pool room and a downstairs bathroom. Dmitri opened some double glass doors. The visitors couldn't believe their eyes when they saw the staircase. It was an exquisite winding staircase, all the way up to the fifth floor. It was made entirely of dark green marble.

Astonished, Harlene asked; "And this is just *one of* the staircases?!"

"Yes, there are four total. The north, the south, the east, and west staircases" said Victor.

"But. This is the only one made of marble" said Erika.

"How did you ever get this house?" asked Hillary.

"I inherited it from my great-grandfather" said Victor.

"Who built it" asked Harlene.

"My great-grandfather's father was the one who built this mansion" said Victor.

"He didn't build it alone, though" Erika added.

"That's true. A man named Innis Hearth helped design the house. He wanted to build it his own way, even though my great-grandfather's father, Percival LaMore, wouldn't let him. So, Innis purposely put several secret pathways throughout the house, so that he could steal things and sneak them out" said Victor.

"When he finally got caught, he was put to death by Percival and stashed away in the attic" said Meredith.

"Why he kept his body, no one knows, but Innis is still up there in *some* form" said Victor.

"That's a freaky story" said Alex.

"I wonder if his ghost is still here?" asked Joshua eagerly.

"Oh please, Josh, Innis is dead and gone forever, and let's just leave it at that" said Hillary bitterly. Hillary, or course, wasn't a fan of apparitions.

Dmitri finally approached the second floor and opened a door.

"Here is the second floor hall" he said.

"And here are the keys to all your rooms" said Victor.

"Each key is marked with a number which is printed at the tops of the doors" said Erika as she handed everyone a key.

"Joshua and Hillary are in room 14. Harlene is in room 15, and Alex and Clair are in room 16" said Dmitri.

"As I've said before, feel free to explore, but, do not enter the doubles door's with the two large S's printed on them. That is my d......, just don't go in. It' off limits to you all, even Meredith, Gabriella, and Eleanor" said Victor mysteriously. Victor and Erika exchanged cautions looks for a few moments, but then lost them.

"Well, see you all at dinner, I'm going to my room to get settled in" said Harlene.

"So are we" said Hillary. Clair and Alex also went to their room.

As Harlene soon got ready for dinner she browsed around her room a little.

"Let's see what's in here" she said as she opened a tall stand-up dresser. Inside hung a red nightgown and a beautiful black and white cocktail dress. They both seemed to be just Harlene's size, and clean too. "Well, I'm having good luck already, I'll wear this tonight" she told herself aloud. Suddenly the bathroom door beside her opened briskly. A man that was Harlene's age wearing a repairman uniform stepped out.

"Oh, sorry, I didn't know anyone was in here" he said. Harlene, being instantly attracted to him, dropped the dress she was holding to the floor.

"It's fine, I wasn't going in there anyway" she voiced.

"Here, let me pick that up for you" said the man.

"I can get it" said Harlene quickly. They both ended up bumping heads together.

"Sorry again" said the man. Harlene smiled.

"I'm Harlene Coleman" she said.

"Maximilian Berry. Call me Max if you want."

"Oh I will…I mean…call me Harley" said Harlene.

"Okay then, Harley, I like that name."

"Thanks" said Harlene bashfully.

"I'm the LaMore's repairman. I travel all over this old place and keep it going through the winter" said Max.

"Oh, was there something broken in my bathroom?" Harlene asked.

"Just the tub's faucet, but it works well now" he said.

"Well, I hope to see you around the castle, Max" said Harlene.

"Me too. Have a nice night" Max replied.

"Bye Max" said Harlene. She watched him leave the room.

"Well, I'm definitely staying here now" said Harlene.

Chapter 8

After a half and hour of settling in, Clair and Alex got dressed for dinner. Alex wore a white tuxedo and Clair wore a beige colored evening dress and put her hair up in a fancy design. They soon came down the staircase and into the dining room. Harlene and Joshua were already there and seated.

"Josh, you look stunning in that black suit, where's Hillary?" Clair asked.

"She's still getting ready" Joshua said.

"I hope she isn't *too* long, dinner is almost ready" said Gabriella. Hillary then came through the door wearing a white dress with large light blue polka-dots on it. She sat beside Joshua and apologized for being late.

Rosario came through the dining door with a dinner cart.

"Enjoy" she said shortly, and walked back into the kitchen. Dmitri then set the food on the table.

"Smells divine" said Harlene. Dmitri went around the table pouring wine into everyone's glasses

"So, what do you do for a living, Clair?' asked Meredith.

"I'm vice president for a company called Lost Hearts" Clair replied.

"Oh really, I've heard of them" said Erika.

"How about you, Harlene?' asked Gabriella.

"Well, I live in Las Vegas and I'm part owner of a casino called The Hot Spot" said Harlene.

"Oh, Sin City eh, I've been there many times to The Mirage" said Victor.

"I've only been there a few times" said Harlene.

"Well, for my part of the story" said Hillary cutting in, "I'm a lawyer in San Francisco."

"Really, well, that's a change. I never would have thought of *you* as a *lawyer*" Harlene added. She poked at the meat on her plate with her fork to get a good grip.

"Some people change, Harley" said Alex. There was a brief moment of tranquil silence for a few minutes until Meredith broke the ice.

"Well, that just leaves Alex and Josh" she said.

"Mine isn't *too* interesting. I'm just a police officer" said Alex.

"What do you mean? You love your job" said Clair.

"Yeah, but, everyone else's seems more…just forget it" said Alex.

"I think working in law enforcement is a great job. My friend's grandfather was a detective until he retired a few years ago" said Meredith as she smiled at Alex seductively. Clair was catching on to Meredith and she gave her a stern look.

"Well, I've been an architect for a few years now" said Joshua, adding to the discussion.

"Have you designed or built any skyscrapers?" asked Erika.

"One, also parking garages. Right now we're working on a bridge design" Joshua answered.

"Oh" said Erika with fake interest.

"Eleanor, do you have a job?" Hillary asked. Eleanor was frozen for second, but, eventually spoke.

"I mostly stay here and keep to myself" she said quietly.

"Eleanor doesn't get out much" said Gabriella.

"I see" said Hillary with confusion.

After the meal was over, everyone was treated to Baked Alaska for dessert. Soon everyone was talking about days when they were teenagers and how much fun they had. Though, on one brought up any topic of Sabrina LaMore.

Lost in conversation, no one noticed the wine glasses starting to slither sluggishly toward the edge of the table by themselves. No one, but Eleanor. She glanced at them a couple times and began to look at the other to see if they noticed. They were all caught up in laughs.

"Perfect timing" she said to herself. The glasses then reached the edge and fell to the hardwood floor. The sound of each glass mimicked that of a gunshot, and made everyone become somber.

"My word!" said Erika with emotion.

"What happened?" Joshua asked.

"I'm not sure, they all just fell" said Dmitri. He went toward the kitchen for a mop, and Rosario came out.

"I better not have to clean that, I've done enough today, Victor!" she bellowed.

"Clam down, Rosario, and return to the kitchen" said Victor as he stared at the floor.

"Alex...look" said Clair. The wine that had been spilled was starting to gather and travel away from the table, forming a small stream.

"What the hell…?" Meredith blurted out, as she saw the wine start to form a message.

It said:

So now, it is time to play

"Oh my" said Rosario with a gasp.

"It can't be" Clair whispered frightfully. Eleanor made a small smile.

"Well, that's about enough for tonight I would think. Dmitri, clean that up. Everyone else, go back to your rooms and have a restful night" said Victor abruptly.

Chapter 9

Later that night:

"It had to of been a freak accident, it certainly wasn't an earthquake that knocked them off the table" said Alex.

"I say it was Sabrina. Victor and Erika obviously know it's her" said Clair as she let her hair down.

"Well...I don't know. Let's just get some sleep" said Alex.

"There's something about Eleanor too, something strange" Clair added.

"Something *strange*. I think you're just tired Clair" said Alex.

"Maybe, but I'm going to browse the house tonight for answers" said Clair stubbornly.

"Don't get us into trouble Clair, it's not your business" said Alex.

"Yeah, but I'm eating and sleeping here. I would also like it if you'd come with me" said Clair.

"I was wanted to sleep, but this seems to be a big deal to you. So, I'll go" said Alex tiredly.

"Good, I'll feel better with you by my side. This place looks horrid at night" Clair said.

Clair grabbed a flashlight and opened the door. They walked out into the hall quietly and began to creep throughout the home.

"I still don't want to do this. I swear this mansion is bigger than Rhode Island" Alex whispered.

"Since when is a tough guy like you ever afraid?" asked Clair.

"I'm not afraid. I just don't want to get caught" Alex replied.

"Whatever" said Clair. They turned a corner and suddenly ran into someone. "Owe!" said Clair holding her dead.

"Most apologies madam, I didn't see you there" said Dmitri.

"We were just looking for a bathroom" said Alex.

"But, sir, there's a water closet in each guestroom" said Dmitri with confusion.

"Good to know" said Clair quickly. She turned around and pulled Alex with her back to their room.

"How are we supposed to search the house with that old freak wandering around all night?!" Clair asked angrily.

"Well, I don't know, or care. Good night" Alex said as he got into bed. Clair went over to the dressing table and started combing her hair in frustration.

"I guess I'll look during the day. This *is* a large house, not everyone can be everywhere all the time" she said aloud, but silently.

Suddenly, there was a soft short tapping at the door. Clair was startled, and put down the comb. She walked over to the door, and opened it quickly. No one was there.

"Hello" she said sternly. Silence. "Hello" she said again. This time with a little fear in her voice. Still no response. She walked out into the middle of the hall. The hall was in gloomy darkness, but lit by a few candelabras for dim light. The only sound was the wind moaning morosely outside the window. Looking back, Alex was asleep on the bed peacefully. Clair shut the door and stood in blackness. She then started to hear faint music. Calm, sorrowful music coming from a piano. Clair played the piano herself, and was quite good. However, the person playing this one was spectacular.

"Who's there" she said with caution. She began to walk down the hall discreetly. When she came to the end, there were some large double sliding doors. Clair could just barely see the bold letters printed across them. Music Room. The piano still played, and Clair slid the doors open carefully and gently.

The room was expansive, with a long row of tall windows. Windows so tall, that curtains could not be hung across them. They went from the floor to the ceiling, and let the moonlight shine magically on a dark figure playing an ivory grand piano. As Clair walked in, the piano player stopped, and Clair was suddenly thrown back against the wall behind her. When she got back up, the figure was gone. She held her chest and caught her breath in deep gasps.

"God!" she exclaimed. She walked briskly over to the piano and stopped in fright. She saw her most extreme fear...blood. It dribbled off the piano's keyboard like, like drool, and made a thick gooey puddle on the floor.

"Ugh!" Clair cried out in disgust, and backed away. The sliding doors suddenly slammed shut with a thundering sound. Clair screamed, put her hands over her mouth, and ran over to the doors. She banged on them to open, but they were apparently locked. The lid of the piano shut quickly, sending a tremendous uproar from the piano stings. Clair ran around in circles with tears streaming down her face.

"Go away!" she shouted in hopelessness. Cold liquidity blood oozed out from the chandeliers on the ceiling and dropped on

Clair's hair and face. She ravaged frantically to get it out off, but got it all over her night gown instead. Pounding and knocking came from every wall in the room harshly.

"Leave me alone! Stop it!" she wailed. Clair spun around and around, until finally hitting the solid, cold floor. She was unconscious, and everything ceased.

Chapter 10

Everyone stood around Clair, as she lay on one of the living room sofas. It was nine in the morning, and no one had eaten breakfast or even thought about anything other than Clair's condition.

"Oh Josh, do you think she'll be alright?" asked Hillary with great concern.

"I hope so Hill, though, she's been out since Dmitri found her earlier" said Joshua.

"Dmitri, would you please go get some ice for Miss Nelson? She may need it for her head when she awakes" Erika asked.

"Right away madam, I shall fetch some Tylenol as well" said Dmitri. Alex knelt down beside Clair and stroked her hair softly.

"Oh Clair, why did you have to search the house in the first place?" he asked her. Clair was frozen and calm, like Snow White in her glass coffin.

"If you don't mind my asking Alex, but why *did* Clair want to *search* my house?" Victor asked.

"I don't remember, I was too tired then" Alex replied.

"Indeed" said Victor persistently.

Clair suddenly woke in a wild daze.

"Blood...Banging...Sabrina!" she yelled.

"Clair, stay calm, you're safe now!" said Alex, holding her steady.

"It's everywhere...Blood!" she rambled.

"Someone has to wake her up!" said Gabriella.

"Don't hold her too hard Alex, I'll be right back!" said Victor. He ran out of the room.

"Blood..." Clair continued.

"Oh my gracious!" Erika exclaimed.

"Don't let her hit anything, she'll hurt herself!" said Harlene. Victor came back and held a lit lighter in front of Clair's eyes.

"Now Clair, stay calm. You were sleepwalking, and you passed out" said Victor slowly. Clair gazed at the flame and stopped moving.

"Good, now sit down" said Victor. Clair did so, and looked at Alex.

"Oh Alex, it was awful! So much blood and pounding!" she said, hugging him tensely.

"I know Clair, you're safe now. It was just a nightmare" said Alex with comfort. Clair raised her head.

"No, it was real, very real! And it was Sabrina!" she protested.

"Wise up Clair, Sabrina's dead and you were sleepwalking!" said Meredith impatiently.

"Don't talk to her like that! She's probably right!" said Harlene confronting Meredith.

"Oh please! She's delirious!" said Meredith.

"I am not, it was real!" shouted Clair.

"No it *wasn't*. There was *no* blood. I'm *not* blind!" said Meredith.

"It was all over the fucking piano!" Clair yelled defensively.

"Go to hell Clair!" Meredith yelled back.

"What about the sounds? Did you hear them, or are you now fucking deaf?!" said Clair cynically. Meredith dove toward Clair in anger. Harlene grabbed her and threw her backwards.

"That's enough! We all know Clair has had a traumatic experience! Meredith, lay off!" said Victor. Meredith ignored Victor and she punched Harlene to get away. Clair then punched Meredith, and she fell to the floor.

"Get a hold of yourself girl!" said Clair. Meredith got up and stomped out of the room.

"Are you alright, Harley?" Hillary asked.

"I'll live, but I can't say the same for Meredith, if I see her again" said Harlene threateningly.

"Just stop Harley, she's not worth the trouble" said Joshua.

"I heard the sounds" said Eleanor delicately.

"You did?' Clair asked.

"How, I didn't hear a thing" said Gabriella.

"You just weren't listening hard enough" Eleanor replied. Her brilliant blue eyes glared into Clair's dark brown ones.

"Eleanor, please, don't look at Clair that way" said Gabriella.

"It's alright mother, I can control it" Eleanor answered.

"Yes, sometimes, but..."

"I said I can control it!" Eleanor shouted, with an instant mood swing. Her voice was strong and dominating, and echoed though the large living room. Gabriella shuttered weakly.

"*What*, exactly, can you *control?*" Clair asked.

"I won't tell you, you'll find out on your own" said Eleanor with a hideous tone. Clair could suddenly feel a slight change in temperature. The room was becoming warmer. Eleanor glared at Clair and gave a short pathetic laugh. She then left the room without a change of expression. The temperature went back to its original state.

Victor interrupted: "Well, anyhow, you should all get something to eat. I'm going to talk with Clair for a few minutes."

"Why?" Clair asked.

"Follow me" said Victor as he started out of the room.

"Fine. I'll be right back, Alex" said Clair.

Victor led Clair to the music room doors on the second floor. The sliding doors were bashed together and fractured.

"What happened?" Clair asked, looking at the doors in amazement.

"I guess when they shut, they splintered" said Victor. "Dmitri and I had to break them open in order to get you out."

"They weren't like this when *I* saw them last" said Clair.

"That's because, you *didn't* see them like this" said Victor.

"What? You've lost me, Victor" said Clair.

"You saw a psycho illusion, Clair, of one of fears" Victor explained.

"It *had* to of been Sabrina then. She's in the house, isn't she?" said Clair. Victor sighed deeply.

"I can't answer that for you, Clair" he said, and walked away.

Chapter 11

Everyone sat around the dining table while Rosario brought out lunch. She served a chef's salad with cottage cheese and raspberry ice tea. Clair felt a little better knowing not everyone thought she was crazy. Meredith, of course, still did. She held a quarrelsome grudge against Clair, and insisted that she had social and mental issues with other people, especially with those who were *smarter* and *a lot prettier* than her.

"Where's Eleanor? I thought she'd be joining us for lunch?" Hillary asked.

"Eleanor wants to be alone now" said Gabriella.

"Does she have many friends here?" Clair asked.

"Eleanor is not a sociable person, she mostly stays here, inside the mansion" Gabriella said.

"Poor girl, she must feel lonely" said Clair.

"Actually, she's quite amused by herself" said Gabriella. Clair gave a flustered look.

"Eleanor is really quite studious though, and keeps herself busy" Erika added. Gabriella raised her eyebrows.

"Yes, she is, but we *don't* always need to talk about her" she said in mild hostility.

"Does she ever leave the house?" Alex asked.

"No, just to the garden out back when the weather's nice" said Victor plainly.

"You know, Eleanor reminds me a little bit of Sabrina" said Joshua. Gabriella dropped her glass alarmingly.

"I...don't think so" she said uneasily.

"I'll clean that up for you madam" said Dmitri.

"Thank you, Dmitri. If you'll all excuse me, I've lost my appetite" said Gabriella delicately, but rudely. She got up and left boorishly, with her hands clasped together in front of her chest.

"It was something I said, I guess" said Joshua.

"Don't worry about it, Josh. Would you like some salt and pepper?' Victor asked.

"Yes, thank you" Joshua answered.

After the meal, Clair found Gabriella in the lounge, polishing an upright piano. Clair walked over to her briskly and slammed the piano's keyboard with her fist, astounding Gabriella.

"Forgive me, and everyone else for being *human* and curious, but what exactly are you hiding from us about your daughter?!" Clair asked coarsely.

"That's none of your business, and if you'll leave now, I have a job to do!" said Gabriella. She turned around to the piano and Clair budged in front of her.

"Maybe I didn't make myself clear!" said Clair.

"I told you all I'm going to say, and unless you want Eleanor to literally *fry* you, you'll leave us alone!" said Gabriella, threateningly. She threw down the dust rag and left the lounge. Clair stood there in laborious thought.

Hillary and Victor came into the room

"What happened, Clair?" asked Hillary.

"We heard some arguing" said Victor.

"Gabriella" Clair said in disappointment. Hillary sat down on an empty loveseat to relax.

"Victor, be honest with me. Is there something dangerous about Eleanor?" Clair asked. Victor paused.

"Well, alright. Sit down" he said. Clair sat down beside Hillary. Victor took out a meerschaum from his pocket, lit it, and began to smoke.

"Eleanor is a pyrokinetic" he said. Clair's eyes widened slightly.

"Please speak English Victor" said Hillary in annoyance.

"She's able to light fires with her mind" said Victor.

"How strong is it?" Clair asked.

"Very" said Victor shortly.

"So, you mean I've been living with *another* person who could easily kill me?!" Hillary asked in dismay.

"Yes. I'm sorry you didn't know earlier. We were hoping you wouldn't notice, but Eleanor made Clair suspicious. I'll understand if you all want to leave" said Victor. He bent over and picked up the dust rag that Gabriella had thrown onto the floor.

"I didn't mean to start anything..."

"You didn't Clair, you would have found out anyway" said Victor.

"I'm sorry, but this is just a little too much for me" said Hillary starting to get emotional. Clair hugged her friend to give supporting comfort.

"Hang in there, Hill" she said.

"If you want, I could show you both something that could cheer you up" Victor suggested.

"What is it?" Hillary asked wiping some tears. Victor smiled.

"Follow me" he said.

They soon came to a large conservatory that was filled with plants, flowers, and trees of many kinds. It was made entirely of glass and came to a domed point at the top.

"Oh wow!" Clair exclaimed.

"It's beautiful, Victor!" said Hillary.

"I thought you'd like it. I planted everything in here myself" said Victor.

"There are so many rare trees! Southern Magnolias, Rhododendrons, Pomegranates, and even…"

"…Coconut Palms" Victor added.

"You even have Cypress' growing here too" said Clair.

"How did you get all of these to grow here? Some of these species can only grow in certain areas" said Hillary.

"Well, Hillary, one thing about me is, I don't believe in the word "can't." I planted what I liked" said Victor.

"What about the Cypress'? Most of them can only grow in water" said Hillary.

"Yeah, and the Weeping Willows need large amounts of water too" Clair added.

"I made additional ponds and customized this conservatory to grow anything inside. I water them with sprinklers, and even have some of the finest gardeners in the world here, working for me" said Victor.

"That's amazing" said Clair.

"I've never seen so many different species of plants together in one area" said Hillary.

"Do you study Botany, Hillary?" Victor asked.

"Oh yes, I've always been interested in plants and trees" said Hillary.

"If you want, you can both go and pick some of your favorite flowers from here. I'll have Dmitri put them in vases in you rooms for you" said Victor.

"Really?! Do you have any hyacinths or snap dragons?" Clair asked.

"What about larkspurs, roses, or calla lilies?" asked Hillary.

"I have whatever you desire" said Victor with a smile. The two women then set off in the enormous garden with joys of feeling young at heart.

Chapter 12

Harlene washed her face in her guest bathroom as she got ready for bed. It was midnight, but she wasn't feeling tired yet.

"I think I'll go walk around the house a bit, just until I make myself tired" she said to herself. She left the room and began to walk down the hall. The house stood in vigorous taciturnity, the kind of silence that can make you seem like you're deaf. Harlene began to count the candelabras in the hall as she walked. It was something she'd always done, count thing, even as a child. It seemed to make her more relaxed in a new strange place, such as LaMore Manor.

"13" she said as she came to a turning point in the hall. She rounded the corner and suddenly stopped counting. She saw two large double doors much like the ones of the music room, except they didn't slide on tracks. She read the bold letters on them.

"Library" she said aloud. She was about to open the doors when she heard a relentless scraping noise coming from around the corner in the hall.

"Who's there?' Harlene asked. The scraping stopped for a moment, then started again, this time with more force.

"I said who's there?!" Harlene asked frustratingly. As the

grating sound rounded the dark corner, so did the figure that was doing it. It was a pallid cadaverous dark creature with no face, wearing a ragged black cloak. It was floating over the floor and holding a large scythe that was carving a deep repulsive line into the wall. The figure was horrifying to Harlene, for it was on of her biggest fears, The Grim Reaper. She gasped in fright and ran into the library, locking the doors behind her.

When she turned around, she saw the large library that was behind her. Wall to wall, floor to ceiling, were bookcases filled with books. The only wall that wasn't covered was the one with windows, the same large tall windows in the music room. Outside, snow came down in a heavy blizzard. In the middle of the large room was an immense round table with several chairs encircling it. Harlene was impressed by this big room. She had never seen such a room like this one.

As she walked by the bookcases she came to a tall, cherry wood, grandfather clock that stood steadfast between two rows of the bookcases. It was aged, and seemed to have stopped ticking years before. Harlene looked at the clock with fascination and then walked past it. When she did, the old clock began to tick softly. It started to swing it's large brass pendulum progressively, like it had just come back to life.

Harlene looked back at the doors she had come through, which were quiet and stationary.

"It must have left" she said, referring to her fear. She sat down in one of the chairs at the table. She sat motionless, not wanting to go back out into the hall. She was alone, or so she thought. Suddenly, a book fell off a high shelf and hit the floor with a short blare. Harlene jumped in shock and got up. She saw the book laying behind her. It was an old thick book with a frayed black and gray cover. Harlene picked it up. At first, it was ponderous and almost made Harlene drop it. She read the word on the cover that was in white lettering.

"Demonology" she said. She glared at the book with bafflement, and then opened it. As she turned the pages, she came across The Grim Reaper, which startled her and made her throw the book onto the table fiercely.

"I've had enough of this" she said as she walked hurriedly toward the doors. Unexpectedly, the grandfather clock started chiming. The sound of the clock's chime was clamorous and brawny, telling Harlene, she wasn't alone. A strong gust surrounded the room. Books flew from the shelves rapidly, hitting Harlene and the table furiously in circles. She was frightened. She flailed her arms at the books and started to become dizzy. She moved slowly toward the doors to escape, but fell to the floor in vertigo. With the loud roar of the wind, and the pounding of the books hitting everything, she still remained determined to open the doors.

As she reached up for the door lock, a book slammed against the doors, breaking three of her fingers. She grasped her hand in pain and then quickly unlocked the doors with her other hand.

"I know you're here Sabrina! Show yourself you fucking bitch!" Harlene demanded. She stood up and a trio of flying books crashed into her head. Harlene fell to the floor, again, this time unconscious. When this happened, every book stopped quickly in mid air, and fell aimlessly.

Chapter 13

The next morning, everyone except for Meredith sat in the lounge with Harlene laying on the loveseat. Dmitri brought in a warm cloth and put it on Harlene's forehead. Hillary paced back and forth with worry.

"I don't know how much more of this I can take. We've got to search the house and see if Sabrina *is* attacking us" she said.

"This is a big house, Hillary, we'd all have to split up" said Joshua.

"I don't care, unless you want me to be attacked and you to carry me home, we'll look!" Hillary said sternly. Meredith suddenly came into the room, since she had heard talking voices. She looked at Harlene.

"God! Not another one!" she said sarcastically. Clair got up from her chair she was sitting in.

"Would you like to lose your teeth, Meredith?!" she asked defensively.

"Just try it, Clair. I'll knock you to next week!" Meredith said annoyingly. Clair didn't move, she just laughed rudely at Meredith's pathetic comeback.

"Do we really have to act like children?" asked Erika in

disappointment. Harlene woke up. She sat up slowly and looked around the room.

"Harlene, are you alright?" Victor asked.

"Yes, I think so" she said holding her head.

'Who attacked you? asked Alex.

"You wouldn't believe me if I told you" said Harlene sadly.

"Got that right" Meredith chimed in.

"Just tell us" said Erika softly.

"No" Harlene replied dryly.

"It's alright, I'll believe you, Harlene" said Victor.

"The Grim Reaper...no...Sabrina" Harlene answered embarrassingly.

"What...did *I* hear right?" Meredith asked in sarcasm.

"Shut up, Meredith!" said Gabriella.

"The Grim Reaper?" Victor asked in confusion.

"It's one of her fears, she told me about it years ago" Clair added.

"I can control that fear easily, until I see it" said Harlene.

"So, you saw it in the library?" Erika asked.

"No, in the hall, outside of the library" said Harlene.

"Whatever, she's messed up" said Meredith rudely. Harlene got up.

"Fine then bitch! I'll show you the wall!" she shouted.

"Show me what?!" Meredith asked.

"The line!" Harlene answered.

"Harlene, what line?" asked Victor. Harlene turned around.

"Didn't you see it?" she asked.

"Probably not, because it's not there!" said Meredith with instigation.

"You're headin' the right way to eating my fist!" yelled Harlene.

"Bring it on *Harley*!" said Meredith.

"I saw the line, Harlene, I believe you" said Eleanor blandly. Harlene fixed her attention on Eleanor.

"When?" she asked.

"I saw the line, Harlene, I believe you" Eleanor repeated abstrusely. Harlene looked at Eleanor with perplexity.

"Are you...okay?" she asked.

"Eleanor, show us the line" said Victor. Eleanor got up from her seat and walked out of the lounge tediously, like she was in a trance.

"That girl is really unusual" said Alex.

"You have no idea" said Gabriella.

Everyone followed Eleanor cautiously up the stairs to the third floor.

"Right there" said Eleanor pointing to the wall. Victor looked at the line in amazement and ran his fingers over the groove.

"That's it, The Grim Reaper was slicing the wall with a scythe" said Harlene.

"Oh please, for all we know, you could've carved that yourself!" said Meredith.

"No...she didn't. Whatever made this line...was strong" said Victor. Clair walked over toward the library's doors and opened them carefully. Books lay scattered everywhere inside.

"If you don't mind me saying sir, when I found Miss Coleman in the library, I noticed that your old grandfather clock started ticking again" said Dmitri.

"Don't be foolish, Dmitri. That clock has been broken since 1982" said Erika.

"It was what I saw madam" Dmitri said profoundly. Victor went into the library and saw the clock ticking steadily.

"Sabrina" he said to himself. Clair glanced at him.

"We've got to do something about this, it's getting worse" she said. Victor looked at Clair and nodded in agreement.

"Tell everyone I said to go downstairs to the living room, we have a house to search" he said. Eleanor smiled balefully as she listened to Victor's words.

Chapter 14

"This is how it's going to work. Everyone will have a partner" said Victor.

"A partner for what?" Meredith asked.

"We're searching the house to find my daughter" said Victor.

"Are you sure that's wise?" asked Gabriella.

"I for one agree. We can't have another person attacked" said Joshua.

"Everyone in the house will help out. I want you all to write your name on a piece of paper, and then we'll put them in something and draw for partners" said Victor.

"What if I don't *want* to participate in your little *treasure hunt*, Victor?" Meredith asked immaturely.

"Then I'll have no choice but to blame *you* for the attacks" said Victor.

"What?!" said Meredith in shock.

"Victor, Meredith didn't hurt anyone, she's my *sister* for god's sake!" said Erika coldly.

"Well, then she can stop being a little wise ass, and help us like an adult" Victor replied. Erika gave a disgusted sigh.

"That is so low of you!" she said.

"It's nothing but the truth, Erika, and *you* know it" said Victor.

Rosario and Maximilian suddenly came into the room.

"What's going on, I was just repairing a light socket in the kitchen, when I was told to come here" said Max.

"Have a seat please" said Victor.

"Everyone, this is Mr. Maximilian Berry, he's our repairman" said Erika.

"We've already met" said Harlene with a gentle smile.

"So, you live here too?" Alex asked.

"Yes" Max answered.

Victor gave everyone a piece of paper and then put them in a small basket after they wrote their names. He then looked over the names everyone held.

"These are the results: Alex and Rosario, Erika and Hillary, Joshua and Gabriella, Harlene and Max, and Dmitri and I. Since Clair, Meredith, and Eleanor are left, all three of you are partners" said Victor.

"Oh, swell" said Meredith disgustedly.

"We should all be adults about this, and leave the past behind us, Meredith" said Victor.

"Where should we all start at?" Joshua asked.

"Wherever you want. We'll all meet back in the front hall in an hour" said Victor.

"*I* don't have a watch" said Meredith shortly.

"Then take the mantle clock off the fireplace with you" said Victor sarcastically. Meredith folded her arms in frustration and Harlene gave a short chuckle. Everyone left the room in all directions, and the search began.

Chapter 15

"We should start off by checking the ballroom" Clair suggested.

"Who made *you* the leader?!" Meredith asked roughly.

"Don't even *think* about giving me a hard time" said Clair raising her voice.

"*Oops,* I think I've upset her" said Meredith mockingly.

"What exactly is your problem?" Clair asked sternly.

"To be perfectly frank, I don't like you!" Meredith answered.

"Get over it! You have to help search the house" said Clair.

"Not to be rude, but I think Clair is more of the adult in this argument" said Eleanor gently.

"Thank you, Eleanor" Clair answered. Meredith looked at Eleanor grimly. Eleanor didn't react to Meredith; she simply walked over to the ballroom's doors and opened them humbly.

"We should start in the attic, then work our way down" said Rosario.

"Do you have any flashlights?" Alex asked.

"No, but we can use the candles from the dining table" Rosario suggested. Alex nodded and went into the dining room.

He soon came back with two slender green colored candles that were placed into small candle holders.

"They were already lit, so I just grabbed them" said Alex, handing one to Rosario. They started up the staircase.

"Do you like working here, Rosario?" Alex asked.

"Yes, the LaMore's treat me well" Rosario answered.

"How long have you been a maid?" Alex asked.

"I've been working here since Sabrina was two years of age. As my former job, I was a detective in Moscow, Russia" she said.

"Really? How come you became a maid?"

"One of my best friends died from a careless bank robber, he shot him. His name was Dexter. I worked with him for a while. After his death, I quit, and came to America. Life as a maid is more relaxing. Although, after meeting Sabrina, I think I would like to retire from *all* types of work" Rosario explained.

"I don't blame you; Sabrina is an emotionally unstable person. I've seen what she can do" said Alex.

"So, how have you been getting along here?" asked Max.

"Fine, just a few disagreements with Meredith" said Harlene. She was staring at Max lovingly.

"Where should we start looking?' Max asked.

"Anywhere's fine, as long as I'm with you" said Harlene kindly.

"Has anyone ever told you that your hair is very beautiful, it reminds me of the yellow daffodils in the spring" said Max. He seemed to be falling into Harlene's charm.

"Thank you, I do the best with its appearance" said Harlene.

"Let's check the billiard room first, and then we'll go to the garden out back" said Max.

"Have you been in the conservatory yet, Hillary?" Erika asked.

"Yes, Victor took Clair and I there for some flowers. I didn't see the whole thing though" said Hillary.

"Alright then, we'll start there" said Erika.

"I actually hope we *don't* find Sabrina here, I may have a heart attack if we do" said Hillary. Erika laughed lightly.

"Don't worry, she hasn't come back yet, so she probably won't at all" she said.

"What makes you so sure? And how come you're acting so brave?" Hillary asked.

"It's my defense mechanism, I also don't want to find her" said Erika.

"I see" said Hillary.

"I hope Eleanor doesn't get upset" Gabriella said to herself.

"Victor told us about your daughter's ability, so you don't have to talk to yourself about her anymore" said Joshua. Gabriella was stunned.

"Then, you know she can easily bring down this mansion in flames" she said.

"Yep. I knew she reminded me of Sabrina somehow" said Joshua.

"The attack at the movie theater" said Gabriella.

"How'd you know?" Joshua asked.

"Victor told as about New York. In my opinion, I think she should have died when the lightning struck her. It would have cleared up many problems" said Gabriella. Joshua looked down at the floor, he thought Gabriella was uncivil to say such a cruel thing. After all, Sabrina *is* a human, and every human deserves another chance. Don't they?

"Let's go look in the basement" he said, changing the subject.

"Well, I guess, but I really don't like basements" said Gabriella.

"Why?" Joshua asked easily.

"The windows are small, and there's only one way out" Gabriella explained.

"We don't have to go down there, if you don't want to" Joshua said.

"I'll go, just not for very long" said Gabriella.

"Okay then" said Joshua.

"Well, sir, there was nothing in the study room" said Dmitri.

"Let's go to the music room. I never really got a good look at it after Clair was attacked" said Victor.

Chapter 16

"Well, here it is" said Rosario as she opened the old creaky door. On the other side was a high constricted staircase with one candle holder half way up to another door. "As we go up, light the candelabra on the wall. We'll need it for extra light when we come back down" said Rosario.

"When was the last time anyone was up here?" Alex asked.

"I'm not sure. "I've only been up there once myself, but, only to look inside" said Rosario. They started up the stairs with Rosario in the lead. Alex lit the small candelabra as told, and entered the attic. The attic itself was extremely large and dismal. It covered most of the house. Boxes, old heirlooms, and porcelain figurines lay everywhere. It was packed. Long and compressed walls with some slanted ceilings made up the general design, giving the room a natural interred feeling. Alex set his candle on one of the boxes and observed an old jack-in-the-box. It was big, and of old design. Its colors were faded, giving it a frail complexion.

"Does this still work?" Alex asked.

"Possibly. I haven't seen that thing is years, not since Erika took it from Sabrina" said Rosario.

"Why'd she take it from her?" Alex asked.

"For being insolent, Sabrina was just beginning to use her powers to get her own way" Rosario explained.

"How old was she at the time?" asked Alex.

"Nine" Rosario replied.

"So, Erika just left it up here, and never gave it back?" Alex asked.

"Correct. I think she was too hard on the child" said Rosario.

"I agree. That could possibly be one of the many reasons she's not happy" said Alex.

"I assumed Victor would have given it back to Sabrina, but, he became like Erika, mistrustful to his daughter" said Rosario.

"Did this happen more than once?" Alex asked.

"Yes, but, eventually, Sabrina became tired of it. She caught on to them, and put matters into her own hands" Rosario explained.

"So, that's *really* what made Sabrina attack her mother" said Alex.

"Yes, Victor probably lied to you" said Rosario.

Victor and Dmitri entered the music room and turned on the lights.

"Set down the candles on the side table Dmitri, I'll need your help to look around for anything suspicious" said Victor. Dmitri did so, and followed Victor over toward the ivory grand piano.

"I don't see any blood stains from Miss Nelson's attack, no anywhere else. It's obvious now, Sabrina made an illusory trick on her" said Dmitri.

"Yes, but not really a trick, Sabrina entered Clair's mind purposely" said Victor. Dmitri gazed at the piano.

"That's quite unusual sir" said Dmitri in confusion.

"What is?" Victor asked.

"When I found Miss Nelson after her attack, the piano's lid was down. Now, it's back up" said Dmitri.

"Are you sure? Maybe *you* put it back up" said Victor.

"I'm positive sir, I never miss a thing. I didn't have time to put it back up, Miss Nelson was badly hurt" Dmitri admitted.

"Someone else did then" said Victor.

"I hope I'm wrong, sir, but it could have been Miss LaMore herself" said Dmitri.

"Yes, Sabrina is the only one who, besides me, that can teleport" said Victor.

"You did say yourself, sir that your teleporting ability is wearing out" Dmitri added.

"It is. It's much too weak for me to travel to another room now" said Victor. "I think it's because I'm getting older."

"I'm still amazed by this greenhouse, it reminds me of a botanical garden" Hillary said.

"It *is* beautiful. Sometimes I come here to relax and clear my mind" said Erika. They followed a stone path in peaceful forest bliss until they came to a small clearing hidden behind a circular wall of many weeping willows bunched together. In the clearing, was a dazzling white marble water fountain that shot out sparkling clear water into the air. The general base of the fountain was a pool of water that also had a marbleized bench encircling the shape of it. "This is the spot where I come to" said Erika. She sat down on the marble bench and ran her fingers through the water lightly.

"This fountain looks more expensive than my house" said Hillary with small amazement. Erika laughed.

"It probably is. I actually thought the greenhouse didn't really need it, but Victor loved the idea and bought it anyway" said Erika. Hillary sat down beside her.

"Do you like living a life of luxury?" she asked.

"Yes, but, sometimes Victor over does things. He likes to buy just about anything and everything" said Erika.

"What about Sabrina?"

"She loves luxury. Though, sometimes, I noticed her being very unhappy. Victor kept buying things for her, but, she didn't always care" said Erika.

"She probably just wanted attention in a different way, from both of you" said Hillary.

"That's what I told Victor, but he obviously didn't listen to a word I said" said Erika coldly.

"Well, I agree. No one can *buy* love and happiness" said Hillary. Erika smiled.

"It's nice to have someone to talk to, someone other than my sister Meredith" she said.

"I guess Meredith isn't much of a helper then" Hillary assumed.

"Right, nor a sister. She's always been a little hot-head and wanted everything to revolve around her" said Erika.

"Who is older?" Hillary asked.

"I am, and she hates it. She also is jealous of me, because I found someone to love and marry. She hasn't" Erika explained.

"Typical little sister. My younger sister, Annabelle, always acted in that similar way, but eventually grew out of it" Hillary said.

"Meredith *hasn't* grown out of it" Erika added.

Joshua and Gabriella walked down the steps discreetly as they entered the basement. It was dark and unsanitary with a musty smell. It seemed to look like a dungeon, rather than a common basement. Joshua reached up at a dangling string and pulled it. A line of lights came on with a short buzzing sound. Gabriella stood on the stairs, cowering.

"You can come down here too, I'm not looking by myself" said Joshua.

"I know! Just be patient" said Gabriella shortly. She put one foot in front of her and fell pointlessly onto the floor.

"Are you alright?" Joshua asked in mild frustration.

"I'll be fine, just shut up" said Gabriella sternly. Joshua left her there and began to snoop around. Gabriella dusted herself off and pretended she was okay. She sat down on a nearby box and peered around.

"I'll bet you've never been down here" said Joshua mockingly. Gabriella straightened her face.

"No, I haven't. I told you I don't like basement, but you made me come down here" she said.

"I didn't make you, you just don't want to be alone" said Joshua. Gabriella was stunned. Joshua was right. She never really liked being alone, especially with her daughter, Eleanor.

Maximilian opened the door to the billiard room and walked in with Harlene. The room was fairly new looking and was a little smaller than the dining room. In the middle, was a large pool table with billiard balls already set to play a game of pool. On the right side of the room was a small bar with several drinks lined together behind it on a shelf. On the left, was a zebra skin couch with black throw pillows and a tall brass floor lamp. At the far end of the room was the only window. A large rectangular bay window with maroon colored curtains.

"I like this room, it has style" said Harlene as she sat down on the pool table.

"Victor comes here every night after dinner to play pool with any challenger" said Max.

"I play pool too" said Harlene.

"Really? So do I. Victor wins against me every time, though" said Max. Harlene smiled and then looked at the drink bar.

"What a drink?" Max asked.

"You read my mind. I'll have a Bloody Mary" Harlene answered. Maximilian went over to the bar and made Harlene's drink.

"How long have you been working here, Max?"

"A few years" he said.

"Do you like it here?"

"It's alright. The LaMore's are nice, and pay a lot of money too" said Max.

"I've always wanted to live in a mansion like this. It's everything I expected it to be" said Harlene. Max gave Harlene her drink and sat down on the zebra couch. Harlene slid off the pool table and sat down beside him.

"Are you married, Max?" she asked.

"No, I live alone" he said.

"Any girlfriends?"

"No, I'm not seeing anyone" Max answered shyly.

"Would you like to have coffee with me sometime?" Harlene asked.

"I like coffee, sure" he said. Harlene smiled, took a big gulp of her drink, and spilled it down her dress.

"Oops, sloppy me" she said in embarrassment.

"Here, let me help you get cleaned up" said Max. He got up and grabbed some napkins from the bar counter.

"Thanks" Harlene said.

Chapter 17

The house stood strong and still as everyone searched around. The outside was beginning to get dark as the evening approached with heavy amounts of snow accumulating on LaMore Manor. Everyone's attention was soon drawn to the front door suddenly, as the doorbell rang once. It echoed through the halls of the house with a harrowing feeling.

"Who could be here at *this* hour?" Erika asked.

"I don't know, but I want to know" said Victor. Dmitri opened the door. Outside, stood a woman and a young girl. The woman was some-what tall with short brown hair, and wearing a dark purple dress with a blue coat. She looked about twenty four years old. The girl, was short, but looked almost thirteen. She had the same color hair, which was longer than the woman's. She held her hands behind her back, wore black rimmed glasses, and had on a blue and pink dress with a white ribbon in her hair.

"Yes madam?" Dmitri asked.

"I'm sorry. I didn't mean to disturb everyone, but my car died a few blocks away. My daughter and I came here, because nobody else would help us" said the woman.

"That's alright, you can come in and warm yourselves for a while" said Victor.

"Thank you. My name is Jill Bridges, and my daughter's name is Kimberly" said the woman.

"Welcome to our home" said Erika. She greeted the woman by shaking hands. Meredith stared at Jill and Kimberly intently.

"You won't be staying here all night, just to get warm and use the phone" she said rudely.

"That's all we planned on" said Jill with caution. Meredith walked away.

"You'll have to excuse Meredith, she's not exactly a *friendly* person" said Harlene.

"That's putting it mildly" Alex added.

"Can I use your bathroom?" Kimberly asked.

"Sure, Dmitri will show you where it is" said Erika.

Victor led everyone to the lounge, and Jill sat down in a vacant chair.

"Do you live here in town, Jill?" Gabriella asked.

"No, I'm from New Jersey" said Jill.

"Really, my sister, Meredith, use to live in Neptune, New Jersey" said Erika. Dmitri soon came back with Kimberly, carrying an old fashion porcelain tea set on a silver tray. Kimberly sat down on another chair, beside her mother.

"Would anyone like some tea? It's an old Japanese remedy, and peppermint flavor" asked Dmitri.

"I'll have some, if you don't mind" said Jill.

"Me too" Joshua added. Clair walked over to Victor.

"How are we supposed to search the house if *those* people are here?" she asked quietly.

"Give me time think of something" answered Victor.

Suddenly, the door opened and Eleanor walked in casually. Her eyes met up with Jill and Kimberly's quickly.

"Hello, Eleanor. This is Jill and Kimberly" said Gabriella.

"We've already met" said Eleanor blandly. She turned around and walked back out.

"How do you know my daughter?!" Gabriella asked stunningly.

"She must be mistaken. As I've said before, we're from New Jersey" Jill answered.

"Yeah, I've never seen her before" Kimberly added.

"Well, I don't believe you!" said Gabriella angrily.

"That's your problem then" said Jill flatly. Gabriella was shocked.

"I want you to leave, now!" she said, pointing toward the door.

"Gabriella, don't be so defensive" said Victor.

"I have the right to. They know my daughter without me knowing!" Gabriella shouted.

"I really don't know her" said Jill hastily.

"Prove it" said Gabriella bluntly. Victor went over to Gabriella and motioned her to leave.

"No" she said instantly.

"Maybe *I* should leave" said Jill.

"You don't have to. Gabriella, please leave the room" said Erika. Gabriella was quiet for a moment, but eventually walked out and slammed the door behind her.

Chapter 18

Since the surprised guests interrupted the house search, everyone except for Jill and Kimberly, were in the dining room pondering on what to do.

"Mind if I smoke?" Harlene asked.

"No, go ahead" said Victor. Harlene took out a pack of Misty's from her purse.

"Smoking is such a *dirty* habit" Meredith said scornfully. Harlene ignored Meredith facilely.

"Did anyone see anything unusual?" Erika asked. Everyone said no.

"*I* figured out something" said Alex.

"What?" Clair asked.

"I'll tell you later on tonight" said Alex.

"Is is really *that* personal?" Victor asked.

"In a certain way, yes" Alex answered truthfully. The mantle clock on the fireplace chimed for midnight.

"I suggest we all get some sleep now. We'll search more tomorrow" said Victor.

"What about Jill and Kimberly? What will they do?" Gabriella asked.

"They can sleep in a guestroom, it's much too late for them to leave now" said Erika. Victor agreed.

"Dmitri, take them to their room, please" he said.

"Are you sure we should have them here? They could be murderers" said Meredith coldly.

"Stop dramatizing everything, Meredith" said Victor shortly.

"If they are murderers, then *you'll* be the first one they'll kill" Harlene added. Meredith stared at Harlene insultingly. Hillary chuckled at Harlene's comment.

"Well, goodnight everyone" said Rosario, as she left the room. Maximilian walked over to Harlene and stood beside her.

"Ready to go upstairs?" he asked her.

"Yep" said Harlene quickly. They both left the room together.

"Well, we better not bother *them* tonight" Clair said surprisingly.

"You people all disgust me!" said Meredith. She was revolted and left the room as well. Everyone else said their goodnights and traveled off to their rooms.

Soon after hearing the story of Sabrina and her jack-in-the-box from Alex, Clair felt some mild anger toward Victor and Erika.

"I would never do that. He should have given it back" said Clair.

"Well, maybe they've changed now that their daughter is gone" said Alex.

"*Maybe*" said Clair.

"Josh, I don't think I can stay here anymore" said Hillary.

"You'll be fine Hillary. You're a lawyer, you *can* handle pressure" said Joshua.

"This is something completely different than winning a case. You remember what happened when we were seventeen, Sabrina is older now and probably more vicious" said Hillary.

"You're right, but, Sabrina hasn't showed herself yet. So, she probably won't at all" said Joshua.

"How do you know? Sabrina had *always* caught us by surprise. Who's to say she won't again" said Hillary. Joshua sat on the bed thinking hard. Hillary was right, and he was just as scared as she was.

"Victor, promise me you'll tell Jill and her daughter to leave tomorrow morning. I'm *also* feeling nervous having them in the house" said Erika.

"Alright, but I still see no reason to be afraid of them" said Victor.

"Let's just get to sleep. It's been a long day, and I don't want to talk about this anymore" said Erika uneasily. She turned off her bedside lamp and climbed into the bed, where Victor was already relaxing. Thoughts were racing through his mind about Sabrina, and the newcomers. Suddenly, he remembered the way Eleanor acted when she saw Jill and Kimberly. He realized that Gabriella was right. They *do* know each other. But how?

Chapter 19

As the morning slowly approached at LaMore Manor, everyone found themselves waking up earlier, as though they didn't get enough sleep. It was seven forty five, and Rosario was already downstairs making breakfast for everyone in the household. Soon they were all in the breakfast room.

On this new day, everyone's choice of clothing seemed to be formal. Clair was dressed in a white business suit and pearl necklace. She almost looked like she was going to give a political speech. Hillary wore a peach colored blouse with an orange skirt. Harlene wore long dangly earrings with her blonde hair up in a bun. Her choice of clothes was a jade green dress. Meredith wore a light blue short dress that was ruffled all around the bottom. Her long light brown hair was down and slightly curly. Gabriella wore a dark red shirt and pants. Her red earrings stood out against her short dark brown hair. Erika wore a canary yellow outfit with a back belt encircling her middle. Eleanor, was dressed in all black, and looked old fashion. She had on a long solid black dress. Her long blonde hair was down and curled all around the ends. Most of her hair, however, was covered by a large black hat, tilted to the side. Last of all, were the men. They all just wore nice shirts and pants.

Victor stood over by the window, staring at a raging blizzard occurring outdoors. Several feet of snow was building up around the foundation of the home.

"Well, Jill, looks like you and your daughter are going to be with us for a little longer" he said. Erika quickly got up from her seat.

"It can't be *that* bad out there" she said. She walked over to the window and saw the storm. The snow fall was so thick, that she could hardly see the trees on the lawn. On the other side of the room, on a counter, sat a little television. A news report was on that said:

"All residents of Warren are ordered to stay indoors. The heavy blizzard has gotten stronger with winds reaching 40 kilometers. Large amounts of ice have built up on the roads, ceasing all traffic flow throughout the city. Strangely, the storm seems to be confined to just our area, while neighboring cities report clear skies. Please stay tuned for more updates"

Everyone watched as the TV station died off in a static frenzy. Rosario turned it off.

"How long can a blizzard possibly last?" Hillary asked.

"Sometimes they can be six hours long, though, this storm has being going on for two days" said Clair.

"How is that possible?" Erika asked. Victor looked back outside.

"I don't know" he said. Eleanor smiled heartlessly at the situation. Gabriella saw Eleanor's reaction. She slid her plate off the breakfast table. The plate of eggs and sausage hit the floor with a crash, and made a distraction for everyone.

"Oh dear" said Gabriella falsely. Dmitri automatically began to clean up the mess.

"You did that on purpose!" said Eleanor rashly.

"I did not, it was an accident" Gabriella said calmly.

"You did it to distract everyone, and get attention!" Eleanor snapped.

"*I did not!*" said Gabriella.

"You just can't admit to it" said Eleanor mockingly.

"You watch your mouth Eleanor Jane LaMore! I don't care if you're nineteen, that doesn't make you my boss! I'm your mother, and you respect me!" Gabriella said defensively.

"Well, I believe you, Eleanor. She *did* do it on purpose" said Kimberly, cutting in.

"What?! You have no say in anything young lady!" said Gabriella fiercely.

"Hey! Don't talk to my daughter that way! I don't care if you're pissed off, you're not her mother! I am!" Jill yelled. She confronted Gabriella in bravery and strong confidence.

"Get out of my house!" Gabriella shouted. Everyone was watching in amazement.

"It's not your house" said Jill boldly.

"No it's not…but it's mine" said Victor harshly. Jill sat quietly. Victor now had control.

"I don't care how cold it is outside, I want you gone" said Erika in a feeble voice.

"I apologize for my actions" Jill said sympathetically. Gabriella walked over toward the door.

"Come with me Eleanor, I want to speak with you" she said.

"No" Eleanor said plainly.

"Now" Gabriella demanded. Eleanor's rage grew. On the

table, a bouquet of carnations in a glass vase started shaking. The room's temperature rose, and everyone could feel themselves beginning to sweat.

"I said no!" The bouquet burst into smoky flames, and the vase exploded coarsely from the heat. Glass fragments from the vase hit Gabriella's face like daggers. She screamed loudly and held her face in pain.

"Oh my god!" Clair exclaimed.

"Dmitri, call an ambulance!" Erika shouted. Victor grabbed several napkins from the table and ran over toward Gabriella. Blood was streaming down her face.

"Keep the blood away from her eyes!" Harlene warned.

"She's lucky eyes aren't cut" said Joshua with concern.

"Damn you, Eleanor!" said Meredith. Eleanor said nothing, and simply left the room.

"Doesn't she have any remorse?" Hillary asked.

Alex got up and helped Victor pull out the glass pieces from Gabriella's face. Hillary started crying at the whole situation.

"The paramedics said they'll try to drive through the storm" Rosario said with worry.

"Where's Dmitri?" Victor asked.

"In the front hall, waiting for them to come" Rosario said. Gabriella suddenly fainted from the pain, and became dead weight. Victor and Alex quickly caught her. Maximilian soon helped, and the three men carried her to the living room with everyone following.

"Does anyone know where Eleanor went?' Clair asked.

"Probably too her room" said Erika.

"I think I'll go talk with her" said Clair.

"Can't you just stay out of other people's business?" Meredith asked rudely.

"*You* can come with me" Clair voiced.

"No, I don't have to" Meredith said.

"Are you *afraid?*" Clair asked tauntingly.

"No...I just don't like Eleanor" said Meredith simply.

"*I* think you are. You should mind your *own* business, unless you're prepared to deal with it" Clair said.

"Whatever" Meredith said, giving in.

As Clair walked through the long hallways looking for Eleanor's room, she suddenly came across the large double doors with the Ss printed on them. Clair instantly remembered when Victor mentioned not to go in the room. Since Clair was so curious, she had an instant desire to go in.

"I wonder what's so special about hiding this room anyway?" she asked herself. She turned the doorknob slowly and opened the door. The room was grand. It had a simple rectangular shape, with windows on the left end. On the right side, was a large aquarium tank, filled with many tropical fish. In front of Clair was a large black concert grand piano. It was so smooth and polished; Clair could see her reflection in it like a mirror. The whole room itself was overly clean and organized. Clair actually felt she might break something if she touched it. Dark red paint covered the walls. A white canopy bed was near the windows, neatly made. The blanket had no wrinkles. On the red wall above the piano, were twelve hand-painted portraits. In each one, was Sabrina holding a different cat. Each portrait also had a name at the bottom. They were the names of each cat Sabrina had ever owned. Each cat name was printed in bold letter on the picture frame itself. The names were: Bright Eyes, Cynthia, Isabel, Lily, Missy, Phoebe, Roxanne, Serena, Raquel, Priscilla, Clio, and Natalie. Clair was very impressed by them. Every picture looked real. Although Clair liked the paintings, it seemed to her, that in every picture Sabrina was staring and watching her every move.

Clair quickly got the feeling out of her mind and began to stroll around the room. Even though everything was so orderly in Sabrina's room, Clair sensed a feeling of loneliness and heartbreak in the room. The room seemed to be a big "show off," and a cover of true feelings in Sabrina. Like a different person. Especially the bed. It was the only thing in the room that wasn't red or black. It seemed to Clair, the red and black was the part of Sabrina that was troublesome. The white bed was her soft side of kindness. Basically, like Sabrina and Clementine. Sabrina, the side always wanting to be adult and independent. Clementine, the side always lost and wanting to be a child. Somehow, Sabrina needed to learn how to be both, at the right times.

Clair suddenly saw something black sticking out of a pillowcase on Sabrina's bed. Clair walked over and pulled it out. It was Sabrina's diary with the silver cat print on it. Clair instantly had a flashback of the time when she first saw the book, back in her school library on the day she met Sabrina. She remembered the table cracking and Sabrina taking the book away from her. She dropped the book on the bed and stepped back, trying to come back to reality. "Get a hold of yourself, Clair. It's just a book" she told herself. She decided to take it with her to examine it later on that night. She tucked it in her shirt secretly, so that no one would notice she had it.

Clair was about to leave, when Eleanor suddenly opened the door and shut it with a loud bang behind her.
"What are you doing in Sabrina's room? It's off limits to you!" she said cruelly.

"I was just browsing" said Clair.

"No, you weren't. You're not going to get away with this" said Eleanor.

"It's really not your room either. I'm sorry for coming in" said Clair. She reached around Eleanor's body for the doorknob. Eleanor quickly blocked her from escaping.

"Sabrina and I are *very* close. She lets me in here whenever I want. But, I can't say the same for you, Clair" Eleanor spoke intensely. Her eyes were solid and glassy with rage. Clair was beginning to feel she was in danger.

"You better let me out of here" she said with little determination and fear.

"No" said Eleanor plainly. Clair could feel her body temperature rising. She was beginning to get a headache. Eleanor's eyes were fixed on Clair like soldier without blinking. Clair pushed passed Eleanor and opened the door quickly. She ran down the hall briskly to get away. The hall was long and seemed to on forever. Eleanor came out of the room.

"You can't hide from us Clair, Sabrina and Clementine *knows* you're here. That's why they've come back" Eleanor called. Her words echoed down the hall toward Clair.

"*You can't hi-ide, you can't hi-ide*" Eleanor chanted in a provoking echoed voice. Clair kept running until she came to a turn in the hall and rounded it. She felt like a child running from a monster in some horrifying nightmare. When she approached the staircase, she ran down them quickly. She soon lost her balance and fell the rest of the way down. She lay on the floor, helpless and unconscious.

Chapter 20

Clair slowly opened her eyes and saw a ceiling above her. Beside her, was Alex, watching over her.

"How are feeling?" he asked.

"I feel like someone dropped a car on my head" said Clair softly.

"The paramedics made it here; they said you'll be fine. Surprisingly, you have no broken bones. Although, you may have a bruise on you head for a while" said Alex.

"What about Gabriella, is she okay?" Clair asked.

"She has many cuts on her face, and she'll most likely have scars" Alex explained. Clair looked out the window, and saw the blizzard was still in heavy progress.

"How long have I been here?" Clair asked.

"All day. Its six thirty now. Rosario brought up some soup and juice for you to have" said Alex. Clair sat up and saw the food sitting beside her on a small folding table. She pulled it over to her and began eating.

Suddenly, there was a knock at the door, and Victor came in.

"You're finally awake I see" he said.

"Yep, I feel fine except for this pounding migraine I have" Clair said, rubbing her head gently.

"I'll have Dmitri bring you up some pain killers. Also, we're going to be starting another search. You don't have to go with us, you should rest if you're feeling light headed" said Victor.

"I'll go. Just as long as my migraine goes away" said Clair.

"Are you sure?" Alex asked.

"Yeah, I'll be fine" Clair answered.

"Okay then, I'm going downstairs for a while and see how the others are doing" said Alex. He got up, kissed Clair on her forehead, and left.

"Clair, I'd like to ask you something. Be honest" said Victor.

"What is it?" she asked.

"When you came upstairs earlier, did you go in Sabrina's bedroom?" he asked. Clair dropped her spoon and it hit the floor.

"Well...yes" she answered.

"Okay. I'm not angry with you, you're just curious. I'm only worried. Sabrina is very *territorial* about her belongings. She would never let anyone in her room. Unless, it was Eleanor. I saw Sabrina's diary lying on the floor beside you. You can look at it if you want" said Victor.

"I ran into Eleanor...while I was there" said Clair.

"What happened?" Victor asked.

"She tried to kill me. I ran out of there and then fell down the stairs" said Clair. She picked up her spoon off the floor.

"*She tried to kill you?!*" said Victor in amazement.

"Yes, and she said Sabrina and Clementine are already here. They've been coming after us" Clair explained. Victor looked out the window at the storm.

"If they are, we have nowhere to go. There's so much snow, the cars can't get out. I don't think it's natural" said Victor.

"Me either. I think Sabrina is doing it. She did this in New York too, on the day I met her" said Clair.

"I also can't find Eleanor, Jill or Kimberly. They seemed to have vanished" said Victor.

"Something is definitely going on between them. We have to figure out what it is" said Clair.

"That's why we're searching again. Finish your dinner, and be ready in an hour if you're coming" said Victor.

"I will" said Clair. Victor left the room without further conversation.

Chapter 21

When Clair entered the living room, she found everyone standing around there, waiting for her.

"Are you feeling better now, Clair?" Harlene asked.

"Yes, Harley thanks" Clair answered.

"We were worried about you all day" said Hillary.

"I'm fine, really" said Clair. She saw Gabriella sitting on the couch. She had several cuts around her face, some with stitches. Her eyes were swelling slightly, indicating she'd been crying.

"Well, now that we're all here, I'm sure you all know what's happening" said Victor.

"Yeah, Gabriella's crazy daughter is missing" Meredith said sarcastically.

"Jill and Kimberly too" Joshua added.

"Personally, I really don't care" said Meredith.

"I think you should be at least a *little bit* concerned" said Erika.

"I'll help look for them, but if *psychopath Sabrina* shows up, I'm gone" said Meredith with a sharp tone.

"Fine, just as long as you help" said Victor.

Everyone got into their groups, and another search started. A thunderstorm had begun, bringing a mixture of lightning and snow.

"That's weird. How can there be thunder and lightning with a snowstorm?" Hillary asked. Erika gazed out the window at the flashing. The lights in the mansion flickered on and off with buzzing sounds. "I hope we don't lose power. This house is so big, you can get lost" Hillary said.

"I *did* get lost once. I ended up spending the night in a guestroom, because I didn't know where I was" said Erika. The lights flickered again, worse than before.

"Do you mind if we just stay here, in the lounge? I don't feel like looking around" said Hillary nervously.

"No, I don't mind. I'm actually relieved you said that" said Erika. They both sat down on a couch, and watched the deplorable storm raging outside.

"We should look on the top floor this time. Maybe we'll find them up there" Clair suggested.

"Okay, but I haven't really been up there in a while. So, if there's something up there you want to know about, I may not have an answer for you" said Meredith. Clair nodded and they climbed the stairs to the fifth floor. When they approached the top, a sudden clash of lightning crackled over the mansion, followed by an extreme roar of thunder. The noise startled the two women, and shook the hallway windows violently.

"That was a *big* thunderclap. I hope the windows don't break" said Meredith said apprehensively.

"We'll be fine" said Clair confidently. In front of them, was the lengthy narrow hall with a long row of doors on both sides.

"Where do we go first?" Meredith asked.

"We'll try them all, one by one" said Clair. The first room, ended up being a common linen closet. As they tried each door, they founded nothing but boxes full of storage. They finally came to the last door in the hall, on the right side.

"This better not be another storage room. I didn't come up here for nothing" said Meredith in aggravation. Clair opened it. Inside, was a large round room with a glass ceiling that showed the stormy sky. No furniture was inside, except for a table with two chair s on both sides of it. The floor was made of solid black marble, and the walls were made of mirrors. The lightning flashes from the storm reflected off the mirrors and gave the room a mysterious show light. The only other source of light in the room, were candelabras aligning the shape of the room.

"Meredith, what is this room?" Clair asked.

"The chess room" Meredith replied.

"Chess room?"

"Yeah, that table has a chess game on it" said Meredith, pointing at the table and chairs. The table was circular, and made of glass. On it was the chess game, also made of glass. The chess pieces were thick and tall. The king itself was at least seven inches tall.

"Victor had it specially made. The black pieces are made from volcanic glass. The white pieces are made from diamonds. On the chessboard, the black squares are onyxes, and the cream colored ones are pearls. The chess game is to resemble different rare elements stones and glass from the earth" Meredith explained.

"It's the most beautiful chess set I've ever seen!" said Clair with astonishment.

"I wouldn't touch it if I were you. It belongs to Sabrina" Meredith warned.

"Who does Sabrina challenge?" Clair asked.

"Anyone. She's won championships, just like her father" said Meredith.

Clair looked around the room slowly. She suddenly saw an old looking door on the other side, between the mirrors.

"What's in there?" Clair asked, pointing at the door.

"I don't know I've never seen that door before" said Meredith. Clair instantly walked over and opened it. The inside, was dark and morbid. The room was gigantic and empty. Clair looked inside carefully.

"Let's go in" she said. Meredith turned on the lights. Large chandeliers lit up the room quickly. It was tall, with the same long, tall windows in the music room and library. As they walked in, Clair suddenly spotted something to her right. When she turned to her right side, she froze in awe. There, stood an enormous pipe organ that went from the floor to the ceiling and side to side. It sat in somewhat darkness with its large brass pipes glowing from the light, giving it a haunting look. Just from the way it stood there, so steadfast and dominant, it seemed to be the soul of the mansion itself. It was shaped almost like an evergreen tree. Starting with the littlest pipes first, climbing in a row to the largest pipes, that were bigger and longer than the world's largest limousines. However, there were large pipes at both ends of all the others, giving the organ an old fashion unique design.

"Holy shit! That thing's huge!" Meredith blurted out.

"I know. I wonder how it got here." Clair said.

"It was probably built in the room itself, there's really no other way it could have got here" said Meredith.

As they stood up against the towering pipe organ, Clair read the words hand-carved elegantly on the keyboard. Property of Percival Sanford LaMore.

"So, Victor's great-grandfather's father owned this?" Meredith asked.

"Yes, at least I think so since his name is on it" said Clair. Meredith shivered.

"This room is freezing. I'll bet no has been in here for years" she said.

"I wonder if it still works." Clair said.

"What, the pipe organ?" Meredith asked.

"Yeah. I've noticed that everything else in this room is old and dusty. Though, the pipe organ isn't. It looks like it's been played not too long ago" said Clair. Meredith noticed too.

"You're right; there is no dust on the keyboard at all. But, I'm sure there's dust all through the pipes" said Meredith.

"Not entirely. When a pipe organ of this type is played, it uses air flows for different sound tones controlled by the keyboard. The wind would possibly clear away the dust in each pipe, especially one of this size" Clair explained.

"That's interesting, but how can you tell?" Meredith asked.

"I can't. I'd have to play the organ and see if the sound is clear or not" said Clair.

"Well, then play it and we'll find out" said Meredith.

"It may be loud, and I've never played a pipe organ before, just a piano. There are many more keys on an organ, than there is on a simple piano" Clair explained. Suddenly, Meredith and Clair were startled by a loud bang that echoed around the room.

"What was that?!" Meredith asked anxiously.

"I don't know" Clair answered. They both walked over to the door cautiously. The door was open, and was swinging back and forth languidly.

"Someone opened the door" said Meredith.

"Who's out there?!" Clair asked. No answer.

"Clair let's just leave this room, and go back downstairs" Meredith said worriedly.

"Okay" said Clair gently. Clair had never seen Meredith so nervous before. She soon realized that even people who don't always have respect for others, can also feel fear.

Chapter 22

After everyone was gathered into the lounge, Clair and Meredith told about their adventure and what they found on the fifth floor.

"*A pipe organ?!*" Victor asked with amazement.

"Yes, it's hidden in a large forgotten room behind the chess room" said Clair.

"Impossible. The only organ we have here, is the small electrical one in the parlor" said Erika.

"I know what I saw" Meredith confronted.

"Well, I believe them. Especially since so many other unexplainable things have been happening here" said Harlene.

"They could be right, Erika, we *do* have many rooms that are abandoned. God only knows what's up there" said Victor. Erika sighed in mild disgust.

"*Could?!* We *are* right" Clair said determinedly.

"We'll show it to you" said Meredith.

"That won't be necessary; no harm came to you when you found it. We'll just take your word for it until we see it later. Right now, we still have to find who we're looking for" Victor suggested.

"Did anybody else find anything unusual?" Clair asked. They all said no. The mantle clock on the fireplace chimed once for eight thirty. Victor walked over toward the lounge's drink bar, and poured himself some cognac. Everyone was quiet. The only sounds were the steady ticking of the mantle clock and the storm outside. Everyone seemed to be lost throughout their minds about the missing people and the possible feeling of Sabrina being in the house. Clair knew there was something between Sabrina and Eleanor. Eleanor was just too brave about being in Sabrina's room. Eleanor, of course, did have her fire starting ability. That, probably made her brave enough to think she could go wherever she pleased. Although, Clair remembered her saying she and Sabrina were very close. Which, obviously meant, Eleanor was the only person Sabrina would ever warm up to without strong therapy.

A clash of lightning struck one of the towers of the house, followed by a roll of thunder. The lights went out for a brief moment, and then came back on.

"I hope you have a strong house Victor, we almost lost power that time" said Harlene.

"I'm not worried about it. My home has stood up against many other storms before" said Victor confidently.

Everyone suddenly started feeling a vibration all around them, throughout every object. It started out very ineffectual, but then grew power, and became highly vigorous by the second.

"What the hell could *that* be?!" Meredith asked.

"I don't know. The lightning didn't really hit very hard" said Erika. She looked all around the room with concerned emotion. The vibrations began to shake the mansion like a small earthquake. Pictures and other objects fell as cracks rapidly snaked through the walls and windows.

"My house!" Victor exclaimed.

"What is doing this?!" Hillary said in tears. Clair and Meredith exchanged worried looks. They knew exactly what it could be. Clair ran over toward the lounge door, and opened it quickly. Off in the distance, and through the halls of the mansion was music. Dull, but controlling and fierce.

"It's the pipe organ, someone is playing it!" Clair shouted. Everyone started running. They followed Clair and Meredith to the fifth floor.

The chords of the strong, mirthless melody, were hitting the hallways like a hurricane's strength. Flowing through the ears of every person in its path. When they reached the room and opened the door, the loudness of the pipe organ's wrath of music hit them like bricks. Everyone retreated by covering their ears. The floor shook, and the chandeliers sung back and forth.

Clair glanced at the pipe organ's keyboard. Jill sat on the bench with her fingers gliding gracefully across the keys. Kimberly and Eleanor stood alongside her.

"Jill, stop playing the fucking music!" Meredith shouted with rage. She walked out into the middle of the room, still holding her ears. Jill ignored Meredith's command. Meredith grabbed a nearby floor lamp, and threw it toward Jill. To everyone's amazement, Jill quickly turned around and then fixed her eyes on the lamp. The pipe organ played by itself. The lamp swiftly darted sideways by itself to the left and was brutally slammed into the wall, embedded in the wood. Meredith froze in shock. Jill, emotionlessly, looked au at one of the chandeliers on the ceiling. The bolts that held it up quickly unscrewed themselves and the heavy light came down at Meredith. Without thinking, Meredith stood there in fear.

"Meredith! Move away!" Erika demanded, in fear for her sister. She ran toward her, but was too late. The chandelier's pointy metal and sharp glass were forced into Meredith's skull on impact. A shower of blood flew into Erika's face as she screamed.

"Oh god!" Rosario exclaimed. Hillary immediately threw up. Victor pulled Erika away. The pipe organ's intense music shattered the windows viciously.

As Jill and Kimberly walked slowly toward their frightened audience, they miraculously changed into Sabrina and Clementine. Sabrina picked up her doll and held it close. Clementine's face had cracks all through it. Sabrina had evidently put her doll's head back together, since the day it was hit by the bullet. Eleanor came up beside Sabrina and they both stood there, staring rigorously. Clair backed away in extreme fear with everyone else.

"Run" said Sabrina in a simple but controlling response. Without hesitation, everyone ran out.

Chapter 23

Sabrina and Eleanor had given them a head start to safety, but would they make it out alive? Alex and Joshua banged on the front doors of the mansion, which were locked tight. Dmitri suddenly burst into flames, as a sure sign that Sabrina and Eleanor were near. Victor tried to put out the fire that horribly burned Dmitri quickly, but couldn't. Dmitri was now dead.

"Let's try the back doors, everything else is locked too!" Harlene said.

When they reached the rear of LaMore Manor, the doors where flung open by Alex. Outside was a maze, which seemed to be made of tall, thick tree-like hedges.

"Victor, what it this?" Clair asked.

"It's the floral hedge maze. There are only two ways out. One is the house. The second is a mystery" said Victor.

"What?! We're running for our *lives*, we don't have time to get *lost*!" Harlene shouted.

"We have to go through it. Do you know the way Victor?" Clair asked.

"No, but Max does" said Victor.

"He's right, but the map of the maze is back in the house" said Maximilian.

"Please, just try to remember. We have no other choice" said Harlene. Sabrina and Eleanor soon appeared down the hallway and started coming toward them.

"I'll try…let's go" said Max.

As they ran through the dark, dim lit maze, Sabrina and Eleanor followed casually but assuredly. They knew the corridors of the maze well. Even more so then Maximilian. Soon, everyone came to a dead end. It was a circular area with a large silver unicorn statue in the middle. With only one way out, the victims were cornered.

"What area are we at?" Hillary asked.

"The dead center of the maze. We're stuck. If we go back now, we'll run into Sabrina and Eleanor" Max replied.

"There must be another way out; you all don't know how strong my daughter is!" Gabriella exclaimed.

"Just stay calm, Gabriella, they may not even hurt us" said Alex.

"That's true, you *are* Eleanor's mother after all" said Clair. Gabriella gave a small laugh.

"That may not even matter now" she said.

Suddenly, everything got very quiet. The storm was no longer raging. A soft, dense mist fell upon the maze. Everyone could barely see their own hands in front of them. The mist was genial, but ghostly.

"Nobody move…they're close by" Erika whispered. They could hear footsteps coming toward them in the snow. Hillary grabbed Joshua's arm in fear. Through the mist, came Sabrina and Eleanor.

"What do you want form us, Sabrina? What did we ever really do to you?" Hillary asked. Sabrina didn't answer. Eleanor began to approach them slowly. The snow on the ground melted and evaporated with each step she took. The unicorn statue had begun to melt as well. Eleanor's eyes fixed onto Clair. She felt her clothes become hot.

"Stop, Eleanor. Sabrina has an idea" said Clementine in her simple innocent voice. Eleanor stopped moving and turned around.

"What for, I can just burn them right here and now. They'll be out of your life forever" Eleanor said.

"I don't want all of them gone" said Sabrina.

"What's your idea?" Eleanor asked.

"Everyone, please follow Sabrina" said Clementine kindly. Since the victims were in a no-win situation, they willingly followed Sabrina and Eleanor back into the house.

Sabrina led them all to the chess room on the fifth floor, locking the door behind them.

"What is it you want us to do?" Rosario asked.

"Sabrina wants Hillary to play chess with her" said Clementine.

"What? I can't play chess! I don't know how!" Hillary said with worry.

"You have to!" said Eleanor.

"I can't!" Hillary exclaimed.

"I will" said Clair, cutting in.

"No, Sabrina has chosen Hillary" Eleanor said hastily.

"I've been playing chess since I was fifteen, I will challenge Sabrina. It will be a fair game" said Clair. Eleanor looked at Sabrina for an answer. Sabrina gazed displeasingly at Clair. Clementine spoke.

"Fine, but if you lose…"

"…I'll break all the glass mirrors in this room, sending several jagged pieces through all of your bodies. Agreed?" said Sabrina cold heartedly. Everyone exchanged fretful looks.

"Agreed" said Clair with confidence.

Sabrina and Clair sat down in the chairs at both ends of the chessboard. Sabrina was the white pieces and Clair was the black. They both were excellent chess players. They both had won championships. Now, they both were competing against each other. The only difference was, Clair was playing for her life, and the lives of others. Since Sabrina was playing white, she moved first. One of her pawns slide slowly to the square ahead of it. It had moved by itself. Sabrina was going to use her power to play. The game had begun.

Chapter 24

Clair moved one of her black pawns two squares ahead. Sabrina reacted by taking Clair's piece. The black pawn rolled off the board and onto the table. Clair just shrugged her shoulders and moved her knight out of line. Sabrina brought out her queen. It moved along the board in a creeping way, like it was alive. It knocked Clair's knight off the board. Clair began to concentrate a little harder than what she was. She had no idea she'd lose two of her pieces so soon. Sabrina was indeed an expert.

"Alex, how good is Clair at chess?" Erika asked with a whisper.
"Good, but I think the victory may just go to Sabrina" Alex whispered back. He was anxious.
"I hope you're wrong, Alex, for our sake" said Erika.

One move after another, Clair lost her pieces. Sabrina twirled Clementine's hair through her fingers as she gazed at Clair's reactions. Sweat rolled down Clair's face. She was nervous and insecure. Sabrina had succeeded on capturing several of Clair's pieces. Clair, however, had only captured four of Sabrina's.

Eleanor watched with fascination. She was obviously impatient to experience Clair's defeat.

"No one has *ever* beaten Sabrina, Clair. You should just forfeit" Eleanor said tauntingly.

"Eleanor is right, Clair. You know what Sabrina can do to you" said Clementine. Clair dropped the chess piece she was holding.

"Why don't you stop hiding behind your fucking doll like a little coward, and come out and face me!" Clair demanded. Sabrina's eyes pierced gravely at Clair. The chess pieces flew off the board in many directions.

"What did you say?!" Sabrina asked strongly. Rage was building up throughout her body.

"You heard me. Come out and play" said Clair with sarcasm. Everyone was stunned. Clair was actually standing up against Sabrina. Clair sat in the chair calmly. Sabrina stood up.

"What the hell does Clair think she's doing?!" Harlene asked.

"She's crazy!" Gabriella exclaimed. Sabrina pushed the chess table off to the side in anger. Clair sat in the chair with fear, but kept her ground.

"You can't shut the world out anymore, Sabrina" said Clair. Eleanor stepped forward.

"Shut up, Clair! You have no idea what life is like for people like us!" she shouted. Sabrina motioned for Eleanor to stop speaking. She then sent Clair flying backwards in the chair forcefully. When Clair got up, she could actually feel and hear Sabrina's power drifting through the air. Sabrina was so powerful, that when she raised her hands slowly and flicked her fingers, every mirror shattered violently. The ceiling shattered as well. The entire room was a storm of flying glass. Victor broke open the door and everyone ran out of the room. Again, they were running for their lives.

Eleanor walked out to the middle of the hall. Her fire-starting power was taking effect, and everything around melted and began to ignite quickly. Eleanor sent large amounts of heat down the hall, causing the walls to burn. The fire raced toward the victims, chasing them down. Rosario was swept up by the flames and fell to the floor on fire. They tried to find a way out, but the halls were like the hedge maze, endless corridors of mystery.

The fire raced along the ceiling above them, and alongside them. The floor gave way and they all fell down to the room below. To their surprise, they landed with a splash, and felt coolness of water surround their bodies. They had landed in the pool room. A small chance of luck that could have easily eluded them. Sabrina and Eleanor came into the room. Clair looked at them helplessly with everyone else.

"I guess you'll never learn" said Eleanor. As Clair waded in the pool, Victor's body floated by her slowly. He had a large piece of broken wood sticking out of his back. Clair pushed his lifeless body away in disgust.

"Get out of the water" Clementine said. Everyone did. Sabrina walked up to Hillary, who was shaking with fear.

"You...will die first" Sabrina told her with a wicked whisper. Hillary shut her eyes, and turned her head away from Sabrina.

"Sabrina, please don't hurt us. We've done nothing to you" said Erika weakly.

"You're wrong, you hate us" said Eleanor.

"I've never hated you, I just don't know how to react around you" Erika explained.

"Bullshit! You're afraid of our powers, you always have been! And now, we're going to give you a reason to be afraid!" Eleanor said.

Chapter 25

Sabrina began to walk around her victims slowly, waiting for them to try and get away. Eleanor was too restless.

"Can we kill them now?" she asked eagerly.

"Be patient, Eleanor" Clementine replied.

"Patient?! I've been *patient* long enough!" Eleanor said. Gabriella glanced at the wall alongside her. Hanging up on hooks, was a fire axe. She had forgotten all about it. She looked at Sabrina and Eleanor. Both were too busy talking to themselves to worry about her. Gabriella slowly reached up for the axe and took it down. She held it behind her back secretly.

"Sabrina, at least let the women go free. You don't need to keep all of us as prisoners" said Alex. Sabrina stopped in front of Alex.

"Would you like to lose your tongue, Alex?" Sabrina asked. Alex shook his head. Sabrina advanced onto Alex and kissed him passionately. Clair's jealousy enraged.

"Now be a good boy, and keep quiet" Sabrina said. Alex was shocked. He did find Sabrina attractive, but he was engaged to Clair.

"What's the matter Clair, jealous?" Sabrina asked scornfully. Clair raised her fist and struck Sabrina's jaw without thinking. Sabrina retaliated by throwing Clair into the pool. Gabriella seized the moment and swung the axe she was holding into Eleanor's side. It cut deep into her body, spilling gushing blood onto the floor. Sabrina saw Gabriella's action and went insane. Gabriella soon found herself flying through the air, and then hitting the solid wall. After Gabriella fell to the floor unconscious, Sabrina ran over to Eleanor and knelt down beside her cousin. A river of blood came from Eleanor's side and ran into the pool. Eleanor looked up at Sabrina.

"I'm…sorry…Sabrina. I wish…it could've been…better…for us" she spoke weakly. Sabrina put her hand on Eleanor's cheek.

"I know. Try not to speak. I'll get you some help" she said in tears. Eleanor's head fell to the floor and her eyes went into a blank stare. She was dead.

Clair climbed out of the pool. Sabrina sat there motionless, staring at Eleanor's body.

"Sabrina?" Erika asked. The walls of the house started to shake and rumble.

"Everyone run!" Hillary shouted.

As they ran through the house, Sabrina threw objects of all kinds at them. They reached the outside, and Clair turned around. Sabrina was coming after them. Everything was under her control. Many of the windows of LaMore Manor shattered. The white limousine parked out front, flipped over.

"We can't just run from her! We need a car! Joshua shouted. Harlene remembered Victor telling her about his classic car collection out in his garage.

"Follow me!" she told everyone.

They opened the garage doors and found several cars lined up. Sabrina stood directly in front of them. Everyone began to run the other way when they saw her. Except for Harlene, who ran behind an Edsel Bermuda station wagon to hide. Sabrina simply tripped her victims with her power, and they fell on the driveway. Sabrina came over to them and stood beside a tree.

They tried to run away again, but Sabrina held them there with her power.

"Let us go, Sabrina!" Clair shouted. Sabrina teleported several knives from the kitchen. They floated in the air and aimed themselves at the victim's heads. Harlene grabbed the keys to the Edsel and started it. She stomped on the gas pedal and drove down the long driveway at high speed. Sabrina was too caught up in the moment of wanting to kill her victims that she didn't the station wagon coming toward her. Sabrina began to laugh maniacally at her victim's jeopardy. Harlene reached full speed.

"Take this bitch!" she yelled. The Edsel hit Sabrina and pushed her into the tree behind her. The knives fell to the ground. The station wagon was wrecked severely, and covered with Sabrina's blood. Harlene opened her door, and got out in a daze. Max ran over to help her. Clair looked at Sabrina's body. She lay on the car's hood with her eyes wide open. Clementine was still in her hands. Alex pulled Clair away. Hillary hugged Joshua tightly.

After Erika had the dead bodies removed from her home by the police, she walked over to Alex with a key. Gabriella was still alive, and had to be taken away to the hospital in an ambulance. Erika held the key out in front of them.

"I'm giving you the entire house. I can't bear to live here anymore" she said. Alex took the key slowly. Without waiting for a response, Erika left them and rode away in the ambulance with

Gabriella. They looked at the house. It stood there grimly. It seemed to be laughing at them, since now they owned the house Sabrina and Eleanor would forever haunt. Over by tree, a police officer was staring at Sabrina's body. He walked over to her closely, looking into her cat-green eyes. One of them moved, and Sabrina's arm rose up to the officer's neck quickly. She choked him until he fell to the ground, dead. Sabrina pushed the station wagon off of her. She saw her victims and smiled sinisterly as she began to walk toward them.

Part 3

Clementine

Chapter 26

Clair Sanderson sat up quickly in her bed with fear. Her nightmare of flashbacks of the incidents at LaMore manor had made her body break out in a cold sweat. After realizing she was in the safety of her own home, she caught her breath and got out of bed slowly. A heavy rain storm had been in progress for a few hours, soaking the outdoors. Clair walked over to her dressing table and opened one of the side drawers. Inside, was the LaMore Manor house key that Erika had given away.

Clair stared down at the shiny silver key with hatred. She quickly picked it up and held it over a garbage can next to her. For some unexplainable reason, Clair couldn't drop the key. It was as if simply discarding the key would never solve anything. Instead, Clair threw it back inside the drawer. Lying back on the bed, Alex woke up and saw Clair standing.

"Clair, is everything okay? What are you doing up at this hour?" he asked.

"I'll be fine, I just had a nightmare" Clair answered.

"Was it the same dream?" Alex asked.

"Yes, but there was more to it this time. More flashbacks are coming" said Clair.

"Come back to bed, you don't have to sleep again. You can always talk to me" said Alex.

"I know, but, I wish I wasn't still having these nightmares, Alex. We still have to raise our daughter up right. I don't want her to see me having problems" said Clair.

"Alexandra doesn't know anything about Sabrina. We don't even have to let her know" said Alex.

"She'll find out someday. She has a way of figuring things out, just like me. It's too big of a secret. Another thing that scares me is; what if Sabrina isn't dead? The police reported her body missing again. It's now a cold case" said Clair with worry.

"I know, but also, we haven't heard from her in years. We should just stop worrying about it and live our lives naturally" Alex said. Clair climbed back into bed.

"I guess you're right, Alex. Good night" she said.

The next morning, Clair poured coffee for Alex and herself as Alexandra came into the kitchen. Alex and Clair's daughter was a teen whose appearance resembled Clair when she was young. Her long dark brown hair was nice and smooth. Alexandra's personality was much like Clair's too. She was eager, audacious, and a quick thinker.

"Did you make waffles, mom?" Alexandra asked as she sat down beside her father.

"Yes, honey, they're on the counter" said Clair.

"Aren't you going on a class trip today?" Alex asked.

"Yep, to the Statue of Liberty" said Alexandra excitedly. Clair suddenly dropped a plate. Shattering pieces of glass slid across the kitchen tiles briskly.

"Clair?" said Alex surprisingly.

"Mom? Are you okay?" Alexandra asked.

"I'm fine, I'm just tired" said Clair.

"Well, did you get enough sleep?" Alexandra asked.

"No" Clair replied.

"Are your nightmares coming back again?" Alexandra asked.

"Yes, but I don't want to talk about it now" Clair said. She put down another plate she was holding and walked away into the living room.

"How many hours was she awake this time, dad?" Alexandra asked.

"I'm not sure, I thought she went back to sleep after the first time she woke" said Alex.

"Well, make sure she takes a nap today, okay?" said Alexandra.

"I'll tell her to, and I'll check on her when I have my lunch break from work" said Alex.

Chapter 27

Alexandra walked with her friends, Josephine, Bonnie, and Delia as they circled the Statue of Liberty. She was concerned about her mother and actually thought her class trip was boring. One of her friends, Josephine, was Hillary and Joshua's daughter. Clair and Hillary both had their daughter in the same year. Over time, and through school, Alexandra and Josephine became best friends. Just as Clair and Hillary were when they were young. Although, when Josephine was born, Hillary and Joshua were still living in San Francisco. They decided to move back to New York City after their car was crushed by a falling tree during an earthquake. Hillary gave up on trying to live comfortably while the ground shook beneath her home. Joshua agreed.

Josephine was very much like her father. Kind of quiet, but willing to try new things and somewhat speak her mind. She had long light brown hair and dark blue eyes. She, however, shared the same fear problems as her mother.

"Wow, the Statue of Liberty is much bigger than what it seems to be" said Bonnie.

"Yeah, I guess so" said Alexandra in a bored tone.

"Are you still worried about your mom?" Delia asked.

"Yeah, she can't stop having nightmares" Alexandra replied glumly.

"I know what you mom's nightmares are about. My mom went through the same thing" Josephine said.

"I know too. She told me about everything this morning before I left. She was also anxious about my safety, and almost kept me home" said Alexandra.

"Is your dad watching over her today?" Bonnie asked.

"He said he would visit her on his lunch break" Alexandra answered.

"Well, then there's nothing to worry about" said Bonnie.

"Yeah, it's not like she'll have nightmares during the day" Delia determined.

"Unless she takes a nap" Josephine added.

"Alright! Just stop talking about it!" Alexandra snapped.

"Well, you don't have to be bitchy about it!" said Delia angrily.

"Sorry, but I just don't want to think about it anymore" said Alexandra. Bonnie looked up at the statue.

"Let's go to the top" she suggested.

"Why?" Alexandra asked.

"Well, we're on a trip after all, and it's not like you can come here everyday" said Bonnie.

"Bonnie's right. We'll have an excellent view of the city from up there" said Delia.

"Fine" Alexandra said evenly. Josephine looked up.

"Can we just go to the crown? I don't want to be on the torch" she said.

"Why not?" Delia asked.

"The crown is safer" Josephine said plainly. Josephine was afraid of heights, just like her mother always is.

"Josie, people wouldn't have built the torch if it wasn't safe to stand on" said Bonnie.

"So, Josephine doesn't like high places, Bonnie. You should at least respect that" said Alexandra.

"I do, but she needs to do things in life too" Bonnie replied.

"We won't be up there for very long, Josie" Delia added.

"Okay, but I'm not going near the railing" said Josephine nervously.

Chapter 28

As they reached the torch, Josephine held tightly to Bonnie's arm without noticing.

"Get off!" Bonnie snapped.

"I'm sorry, but I don't like it up here" said Josephine.

"She's just nervous, Bonnie" said Alexandra.

"Well, be nervous somewhere else!" Bonnie said rudely. Josephine let go and backed away. Delia and Bonnie both stood up against the railing the encircled the torch's deck. Alexandra stood by Josephine to make her feel more comfortable.

"The view *is* pretty from up here" said Josephine.

"I can feel the wind rocking the torch back and forth" said Alexandra.

"Are you sure this thing is safe?" Josephine asked.

"Yeah, it's supposed to move back and forth with the wind. If it didn't, the torch would break in half" Alexandra explained. On the opposite side of the torch, stood a tall, curly haired blonde woman. She was dressed in all white with a matching hat and white rimmed sunglasses. Her long hair seemed it was trying to wrap itself around her neck in the blustering wind. She paid no attention to the others on the torch deck as she gazed at the Atlantic Ocean.

Josephine was starting to get use to the feeling of the torch. The wind seemed to relax her. She looked at Alexandra who was looking around the deck cautiously.

"What's wrong?" Josephine asked.

"I'm getting the feeling again" said Alexandra warily.

"What feeling?" Delia asked. Alexandra had a strong serious look across her face.

"The feeling I get when something isn't right. When something bad is about to happen" she said. The tall blonde woman turned her head slightly as she listened. Alexandra had a special gift. A talent of predicting when extreme occurrences would happen. Clair's mother had it. Although, Alexandra could only tell when terrible things happened.

"I don't know what's going to happen, but I know it's something bad. We should get off the torch" Alexandra suggested.

"I say we stay here. Josephine has probably got you worried" said Bonnie.

"No. We need to get off the torch and back down the statue" said Alexandra.

"She's right. I'm starting to get nervous again" said Josephine.

"You're always nervous!" Bonnie said crudely.

"Stop it, Bonnie!" said Delia sternly.

The Statue of Liberty's torch started to suddenly rock softly. Then started to gain power and shake heavily.

"Get off the torch now!" Alexandra yelled. A strong scale earthquake had started to quaver New York City. The shaking was immense and tossed the boats and ships around in the Long Island Sound. Bonnie held onto the railing tightly.

"Everyone! Come with me down the stairs!" shouted the blonde woman. She had already opened the door and was signaling to go.

"I'm too scared to move!" Bonnie yelled frightfully.

"We have to leave now or we'll die!" said Alexandra. Josephine had already run over toward the door. The steel girders inside the torch and statue started to bend and snap rapidly. The torch deck broke in thirds. One third fell, the other two held up the people. The quake grew in strength and the main base of the statue fractured. The steel made a groaning sound as it bowed and twisted. The blonde woman grabbed Josephine and told her to go down the stairs.

"Let go of the railing, Bonnie!" Alexandra shouted.

"No!" Bonnie cried out in fear.

"Now!" Delia demanded. Bonnie slowly grabbed Delia's arm. The deck broke again and Bonnie fell, pulling Delia with her.

"Oh my god!" Alexandra yelled. The blonde woman pulled her away and started down the stairs. The whole torch pedestal fell off the statues right arm and came crashing onto people down below.

It was horrible inside on the staircase as they descended hundreds of steps. The quake's shaking made it very difficult to walk down them properly. Several individuals lost their footing and either fell over the staircase rail, or partly down the steps. As everyone raced out of the doors of the statue, toward Liberty Park. The quake subsided. Alexandra looked up at the statue. The rest of the famous tourist attraction was now an unsound structure. Alexandra and Josephine both couldn't believe they had survived.

Chapter 29

Most of the city received damage, though, all of the skyscrapers still stood. The blonde woman offered to take the teen girls home. Alexandra felt she could trust the woman enough for that. Josephine called her parents on her cell phone and found out they were at Alexandra's house. They told her to come with Alexandra.

"I hope my house is okay, my mom didn't say" said Josephine.

"It should be. I think most of the earthquake was downtown. We both live in the residential area" said Alexandra.

When they got to the Sanderson home, the teens told their parents what happened at the Statue of Liberty. The parents where instantly relieved their children were safe. Clair noticed the blonde woman.

"Thank you for bringing them here. I was so worried" she said. The blonde woman took off her sunglasses and hat.

"Not a problem for me. I'm Alice Hill" she said, extending out her hand. Clair shook hands.

"I'm Clair Sanderson. I'm Alexandra's mother. This is my husband, Alex, and my friends, Hillary and Joshua Deller" said Clair.

"That's good news to me" said Alice.

"What do you mean?" Joshua asked.

"Well, I'm a parapsychologist. My boss's name is Norman Brownberg. I was supposed to find you all today and tell you some unexpected news" Alice explained.

"What news?" Hillary asked.

"Well, not all of you are here. I need a Miss Harlene Coleman too, in order to break the news. There are two others out looking for you as well. Their names are Mariam Lyson, and Jean Ward. They're also parapsychologists who work with me" Alice explained.

"I'm really not following you. How important is this *information*?" Alex asked.

"Important enough for us to travel several miles to find you" said Alice.

"Can I see some proof you're a parapsychologist, please?" Clair asked.

"Sure, here's my card" said Alice. She handed it to Clair.

"Well, I have Harlene's number if you want me to give her a call" said Clair.

"Please do" said Alice hastily.

"Wait a minute, there's not a down side to this is there?" Joshua asked.

"Yeah, how do we know we can trust you?" Hillary asked.

"Rest assured, we know what you've gone through" said Alice carefully and seriously. Clair looked at Alice intently. "I think you *know* what I'm talking about, Clair" said Alice.

Chapter 30

That night, Clair offered her friends to stay the night at her house. Alice had stayed all day and told everyone the news would be mentioned tomorrow morning. It was disappointing to everyone that she didn't tell about it. During the day, she seemed to want to get to know them better first.

"I wanted to talk to you about something, Clair" said Alice.

"What about?" Clair asked.

"Your daughter"

"My *daughter*? Why?" Clair asked with concern.

"At the time before the earthquake occurred today, I noticed your daughter has a special gift" said Alice.

"Yes…I know she does. My mother had it too" said Clair.

"It's called Precognition. There is obviously a history of it in your family. It could have been dominant for several years before your mother got it. It's strong in Alexandra, I can tell" said Alice.

"I've done some research on Parapsychology myself. That's how I could realize her psychic ability. Though, it rarely takes effect. It hasn't happened for a while now" said Clair.

"When was the last time?" Alice asked.

"She was fourteen. We were on the east New York highway.

Alexandra predicted something bad was going to happen. A minute later, there was a six car pile-up on the highway. We would have been involved if she wouldn't have said anything" said Clair.

"Now, since she's older, she can sense when more extreme things will happen. Like an earthquake" said Alice. Clair nodded.

"Well, enough about that for now. The main thing is what you'll know tomorrow. I suggest you get some sleep. I'll be back in the morning with my boss and two co-workers" said Alice.

"Alright. Thanks again for bringing home Alexandra" said Clair. Alice went out the front door with a wave goodbye.

The next morning, Clair was up a eight o'clock to be ready for Alice Hill to arrive. She found Alexandra in the kitchen.

"Why are you up so early? I said you don't have to go to school today" said Clair.

"I know, I'm just wondering about that Alice woman. Wondering if we can trust her or not" Alexandra said.

"Did you get a bad feeling about her?" Clair asked.

"No"

"We'll be fine. You know your father and I won't let anyone hurt you" said Clair.

"Yeah, I know" said Alexandra.

"Is Josephine still sleeping?" Clair asked.

"Yeah. We're the only ones awake" said Alexandra.

"Not anymore, I woke Josh and Hillary" said Clair.

"Oh...then I guess I'll wake Josie"

In a half an hour, Alice arrived in an old station wagon. A 1972 Chrysler to be exact. It was ocean blue with wood grain surrounding it. Two women and a man also came out of the car. The man was an average height. He wore a gray suit, glasses, and had dark brown hair. He carried a black briefcase in his hand. One of the women had long curly red hair and wore a scarlet colored business suit. The other woman was tall with short black hair. She wore glasses and a dark blue dress. The women also carried their own briefcases.

Clair came outside to greet them.

"Hi Clair. I'd like you to meet Mariam Lyson, she's the red head, Jean Ward, and Norman Brownberg" said Alice. "They were anxious to meet you all."

"Well, let's go inside then" said Clair.

Everyone was seated in the living room. Josephine came down the stairs and was surprised to see the newcomers. She quickly walked over to the dining room where Alexandra had been sitting.

"It's okay, Josie, these people are just here to explain a few things" said Hillary. Josephine refused to say anything.

"She's shy around new people" said Joshua.

"I completely understand. I use to be the same way" said Mariam.

"Well, we better get to the point. As I've said before, we know what you've gone through" said Alice.

"We would like you all to come on a trip with us" said Norman.

"What kind of trip?" Alex asked.

"We'd like to go to LaMore Manor" Norman explained. Hillary dropped her drink she'd been holding.

"No…NO! I refuse to go there! Not ever again!" she yelled.

"Please stay calm Mrs. Deller" said Jean.

"I don't have to be calm!" Hillary voiced.

"Well, then, don't be. At least listen on why we're asking you to go" said Jean.

"Why, you're just going to persuade us to go and then we'll all be killed!" said Hillary.

"Let's listen, Hillary. Maybe there is a good reason for this" said Joshua. Hillary was stunned.

"I don't want to run into that devil child! I can't handle seeing her again!" she said in a frightened tone. Mariam and Jean were both surprised at how frightened Hillary was. They expected them to be unwilling at first, but they didn't really *know* how they'd respond.

"What's the reason for bringing this up? We've been able to live peacefully for a while now. Why talk about it again?" Clair asked sturdily.

"The earthquake wasn't natural, Clair. It was created." said Alice loudly. Everyone froze.

"What?" Clair asked in bafflement.

"Mrs. Sanderson, you daughter was a victim of Sabrina LaMore" said Norman critically. Alexandra was beginning to catch on. The very name, Sabrina LaMore, was horrendous to Clair's ears. She was astounded and scared. Alexandra came into the room slowly.

"Why me?" she asked.

"Not just you, Josephine as well" said Mariam. Hillary got up and went over to her daughter. She hugged her and began to cry.

"Sabrina is a very unusual individual, but very witty. You all already know she's dangerous. She knows Alexandra and Josephine are basically "young Clair and Hillary." She thinks of them as a link to you all, and as "fresh meat." said Jean.

"How can we stop this?" Alex asked.

"I know it sounds very unlikely, but Sabrina must be convinced to have therapy. We need to find out why she has taken such a strong revenge on her life" said Norman.

"Why go back to LaMore Manor?" Clair asked.

"Erika LaMore wants you to come back. She contacted us. Apparently, something very peculiar is happening there" said Alice. Clair was silent for a moment. She looked at her friends, and then at her daughter. They were all tense and serious.

"I'll call Harlene" she said finally.

Chapter 31

Clair explained everything to Harlene that night over the phone. Harlene promised her friend she would come and be there by the next morning. Alice, Norman, Jean and Mariam left. They went to the local Holiday Inn to stay the night. They told everyone to pack what they wanted to bring and they'd be back the next morning when Harlene arrived. Joshua and Hillary went to their house to pack. They came back afterwards to stay the night at Alex and Clair's house again.

"Are you sure you *want* to do this, Clair" Alex asked.

"No" Clair answered uncertainly.

"Mom, I don't want to go if it's going to be a bad idea" said Alexandra.

"I'm not leaving you home, you're coming with" said Clair, ignoring Alexandra. She left the room and Alexandra was speechless.

After Clair and Alex finished packing, Clair opened the drawer with the key to LaMore Manor. She picked it up. The large silver key was heavy and cold as ice. After glaring at it for a few minutes, she put it in her pocket.

Alice arrived at ten the next morning in her station wagon. Harlene had got there by nine thirty. Norman, Jean, and Mariam rode with Alice instead of taking cars they already owned.

"There's enough room in the back of the wagon for your suitcases. You can put them there if you want" said Alice.

"Thanks Alice, but we've already packed some of our things in our cars" said Clair. The Dellers climbed into their little gray Chevette and Alex finished packing in his car. Every car's engine started and everyone was soon off to LaMore Manor.

The drive was long, mostly on the interstate. Occasionally they stopped at restaurants to eat, but were soon driving again. It was not until around seven they arrived at their destination. LaMore manor looked the same as it did the last time they were there. Large, dark and melancholy. Though, much of it had been repaired. One of the reasons it looked so dark, was because of the solid gray stone and terra cotta it was made from. The other reason was because of its ethereal reputation. Alexandra and Josephine were amazed by the large mansion. Though, as Alexandra looked at it, she could sense a ghastly presence upon the house. Clair didn't have the same ability as her daughter, but she too could sense something. There was something new about LaMore Manor, something that gave the feeling of not being entirely alone. Alice seemed more than ready to go in. Norman too. Clair supposed, being parapsychologists, they were rather excited to be here. Jean and Mariam were like Josephina and Alexandra, impressed at how large the house was. It was obviously their first time here too. Alice and Norman had been here before, probably when they met Erika.

Joshua rang the doorbell when they got to the front doors. It was answered by a short young woman about twenty eight with brown hair and hazel eyes. She seemed surprised to see the newcomers.

"Hello, we're looking for Erika LaMore. Is she here?" Clair asked.

"Oh, you must be Clair. I'm Theresa Kain, I live next door. I help take care of the mansion now. Erika is in the parlor with Gabriella." said the woman.

"Thank you, Theresa" said Norman. When they arrived inside the parlor, Erika saw them first.

"Hello everyone, glad you could all make it here" she said.

"Hi Erika, we were told you wanted to see us again" said Clair.

"You were told correctly. Please, come and sit down" Erika said.

Chapter 32

"I wanted you all to come back, because there is something going on in my house" said Erika.

"What kind of something?" Alex asked.

"There is a problem with the house. We all know that Sabrina is not dead. She was able to escape death by her power, telekinesis. For some time now, the mansion has seemed to be haunted" said Norman.

"*Haunted?* By who?" Hillary asked.

"Where not sure. We don't even know if Sabrina is to blame" said Gabriella.

"Well, there *was* death in this house. There's probably a ghost" said Harlene.

"Not really just a simple ghost" said Jean.

"What do you mean?" Harlene asked in confusion.

"The general nature of a ghost is to act like they're still alive. Sometimes ghosts don't realize they're dead. Others times they do. A ghost can't leave the place where they've died either, unless they've died outdoors. This possible ghost of LaMore Manor is no ordinary ghost. It likes to haunt for fun, *and* is able to kill" said Norman.

"How can a ghost kill somebody? They're dead" said Joshua.

"They are different types of ghosts. There is a normal apparition, then there are phantoms and poltergeists. These types can attempt to kill another living thing or even embody them. Something like a demon" said Mariam.

"I don't like the sound of this already" said Hillary fretfully.

"Who could have become something like that" Clair asked.

"Think about it, Clair. We know Rosario, Victor, Dmitri, and Meredith died here. Although, there was one other" said Erika. Clair was silent for a moment. There *was* only one other person.

"Eleanor" Clair said softly. It was blatant. Eleanor was haunting LaMore Manor and killing because she had been murdered. She wants revenge for being killed and not being able to help Sabrina.

"Can Eleanor still use her pyrokinesis while dead?" Clair asked.

"We're not sure, but most likely, yes" Norman said.

"I have question" said Harlene.

"Yes?" Norman asked.

"Every time we saw Sabrina, she seemed to have not aged at all. She still looked seventeen or eighteen, and always wore the same red dress. Why?" Harlene asked.

"Well, as you already know, Sabrina has the ability to make psycho illusions. She wants everyone to only see her as an eighteen year old. That's why she'll look the same as she did when you first met her" Norman explained.

"Does Theresa know about any of this?" Hillary asked.

"We filled her in on everything. Some things were hard for her to believe, but she eventually trusted us when she experienced some of the haunting" Jean clarified.

"What did she experience?" Joshua asked.

"She told us she had seen the kitchen stove and other appliances turn themselves on. Even the lights would go out for several hours at a time, giving the house a dreary look and dejected feeling. When we checked our power line, it was perfectly normal" said Gabriella.

"It was basically some of the same things Gabriella and I experienced" said Erika.

"That's not too surprising. The term "poltergeist" actually comes from the German language, meaning "noisy ghost" said Jean.

"Has anything happened today?" Alexandra asked.

"No, the haunting sometimes comes in cycles" Erika said.

"Well, we should all go choose our rooms and get settled in" said Alice.

"There should be enough room. We have six stories of house with several guestrooms after all" said Erika. They all grabbed their bags and headed up the old spiral staircase made of marble.

Chapter 33

On the fifth floor, everyone chose their rooms. They were all in a row down a long hall. Harlene remembered the feeling of being in the house very easily. A suffocating feeling of unknowingness and apprehension. She remembered the night she ventured out in LaMore Manor and was attacked in the library. Something she always wanted to forget, but couldn't. The same feeling went through Clair as well. The night she was attacked in the music room. Clair thought the trip was going to be easy. She thought wrong. It was like taking a trip back in time. She could see the cracks in the walls from the ungodly pipe organ. It was probably still there; up on the sixth floor collecting dust and having that uncanny look. Clair shook her head to relieve her thoughts of the mental image. Gabriella and Erika were going to each of the rooms, telling their guests when dinner would be ready. Everyone was hungry, and the thought of eating good food released stress.

"Theresa has offered to fix meals for us. She will be staying on the fourth floor" said Erika.

"What's she making tonight?" Alexandra asked.

"The main course is grilled sea bass with alfreado cheese

pasta" said Gabriella. Alex suddenly had a disappointed look on his face. He wasn't a big fan of seafood. Erika realized this.

"Don't worry, Alex, were also serving Swiss steak and salad" she said.

"Thank you, Erika" Alex responded.

Dinner started around 7:45 after everyone was settled and dressed in dining clothes. In the middle of the dining table, was a beautiful bouquet of honeysuckles. It started to rain casually outside as they ate.

"So, Harlene, how are things with you and Maximilian?" Alex asked.

"We're doing okay. Max just got a job promotion at a gardening company. He now works in a large greenhouse with many types of plants. He usually brings home flowers for me every other day" Harlene said happily.

"That's sweet. Think you're both great together" said Hillary. Harlene nodded in agreement.

"How long has Theresa been working her, Erika?" Joshua asked.

"For about a week now. Theresa is the only neighbor that agreed to help us take care of the mansion. Everyone else wouldn't even go inside the front doors for five minutes" Erika said.

"Well, she's a really good cook!" said Jean.

"I don't remember her living next door when we were here the last time" said Alex.

"That would explain why she was the only one who agreed to come here. She's new, and didn't really know about the house's history" Mariam added.

As everyone talked, Alexandra noticed Alice wasn't adding any conversation of her own. She simply sat there eating while the others carried on. It was now, Alexandra got her feeling again. And this time, it was coming from Alice.

"So, Alice, do you like your job?" Alexandra asked her. Alice brought her attention to the girl's question.

"Of course. I love exploring and studying the unknown" Alice answered simply. Josephine now wanted to talk.

"Have you always wanted to do what you do?" she asked.

"Yep. My first reason for wanting to was when I lived in a haunted house for two years. The haunting from the spirits was fascinating to me" Alice said.

"I think it would be very cool to be around ghosts" said Josephine. Alice smiled.

"It is" she said. Alexandra was now confused. Her feeling began to go away. She couldn't tell if Alice was a person that was trustworthy, or to be taken seriously. Alice seemed very comfortable talking about herself, considering it was the first time she had spoken since dinner started. Alexandra decided she'd tell her parents later, but for now, she was just going to ignore it.

Chapter 34

That night, Alexandra did as she promised herself she'd do. She told her parents what she thought about Alice. Knowing about Alexandra's ability, Clair and Alex decided they'd do a little exploring in Alice's room later to see if she was hiding anything. For now, they went to bed.

Now, the mansion was quiet. The quietest it's ever been. No one could sleep, possibly because it was the first night. Clair and Harlene both decided they weren't going to walk about LaMore Manor by themselves like they did the last time. Mariam, however, did want to do some exploring to see what the mansion was like. After she left her room, she began wandering the halls. She had taken a flashlight with her, which she had put new batteries in because the old ones were dead.

"This place is so big, I hope I don't get lost" she said aloud as she rounded a corner. As she started walking down a long corridor, she began to hear a voice. It was soft, like a child's whisper, but provoking. It called out a name. "*Maarriiamm*" She stopped in her tracks. Mariam's flashlight was old and produced little light. She couldn't even see the end of the hallway.

"*Maarriiamm*" it called again. She looked back and forth though the hall. She couldn't see the end of either direction. Mariam's heartbeat began to accelerate. Her flashlight suddenly died. Being a parapsychologist, Mariam knew only supernatural activity could kill fully charged batteries. Not knowing what to do, she began to walk even further. She soon found a door, and opened it slowly.

The room was semi small and dark. The only light came from the moon outside. The window was open, allowing the blustering night wind to blow in the curtains. On the floor, lay many broken toys. The wall paper, with a clown-like theme, was ripped in many areas. By the window in the right corner was a small white bed with old unmade sheets. It was a child's room. "*Oh Maarriiamm...come inside*" the ghoulish little voice whispered. As if Mariam was in a trance, she walked in. The door behind her shut briskly. As she walked over the broken toys she found a large ice pick lying on the bed. She hadn't noticed it before, since it was under one of the sheets. She picked it up and quickly dropped it. It was heavy and made of metal. Mariam left it on the floor and drew her attention to the wall. She was beginning to wonder why it had been ripped so violently. Though, she wasn't about to know the reason why. Mariam had become and unwanted guest at the mansion. Someone didn't want her there. And that someone suddenly picked up the ice pick and swung it into her stomach.

Mariam clutched her abdomen in great pain and fell to the floor. She turned her head and realized no one was in the room with her. She crawled out of the room and down the hall, leaving a long blood trail. The ice pick was wedged deep into her stomach to where she couldn't pull it out.

"Some...one...help...me...please!" she cried out weakly in slurred words. No one could hear her. She was alone. Mariam eventually could not go on any longer, and died in the middle of the hallway.

Chapter 35

The next morning, Clair and Alex were surprised to wake up to a loud banging on their door. Clair was the first one up, so she answered it. When she did, she found Hillary standing there in tears.

"Hillary?! What happened, why are you crying?!" Clair asked quickly. Hillary couldn't speak, she simply cried gently. Alex was now concerned too. Joshua came running down the hall toward them.

"Erika wants everyone down in the living room, apparently there's been a murder" he said. Clair and Alex got dressed and walked with Hillary down to the living room where everyone else had already been sitting. They sat Hillary down with Joshua and Josephine on the couch. Alexandra was standing over by Harlene and Alice.

"What happened?" Clair asked.

"Last night, someone killed Mariam" said Jean.

"It happened in the hallway we think" said Norman.

"How did it happen?" Clair asked frightfully.

"It's too gruesome to say" said Norman, shaking his head in disgust.

"I'd like to look at her body, I'm a police officer and I've done some detective work as well" said Alex.

"Who could have killed her?" Alexandra asked.

"We don't know, everyone was asleep" said Alice.

"Let's go and investigate the area where it happened" said Erika.

"I agree, but I want Alexandra and Josephine to stay here with Hillary" said Clair.

"I'll stay too, Clair" said Gabriella.

"Thank you" Clair replied.

Everyone else then followed Erika and Norman to the hall where Mariam lay in a pool of blood. Her skin was turning a pale color. The ice pick was lying beside her.

"Is this what she was stabbed with?" Alex asked.

"Yes. I checked it for finger prints before I pulled it out. I didn't find any" said Norman.

"What do you mean? If you didn't find any prints, how was she *murdered?*" Jean asked.

"The person could have been wearing gloves" said Alex.

"Or...it wasn't a person who killed her" said Norman. Clair drew her attention to Norman abruptly.

"A ghost?" she asked.

"Possibly" said Norman, nodding. Alex gazed down the hall at the thick wavy blood trail.

"Where does that lead?" he asked.

"I don't know. We didn't look" Norman answered. Clair started walking down the hall leisurely. Everyone soon followed without question.

They came to the small room Mariam had discovered and Clair stared in with curiosity.

"Erika, what room is this?' she asked. Erika seemed to not want to look at it.

"It was Sabrina's baby room" she answered with a jittery tone. Clair looked back in. The room had a dark purpose to it. Clair realized something terrible happened here, even before Mariam's death.

"Did anyone else have this room?" Norman asked. Erika flinched and then spoke.

"A while ago, Sabrina and Eleanor shared this room together" she said. Norman looked at the torn, clown wall paper.

"What it Sabrina afraid of?" he asked.

"I know where you're going with this, Norman. I'm done talking. If you really want to know, figure it out on your own" said Erika rudely. She left the room.

"I suggest we don't call the police, they may think one of *us* killed Mariam. We should put her body someplace and clean up this mess" said Alex.

"I'm going to have a look around" said Clair.

"Mind if I join you?" Jean asked.

"Not at all. You can help me look for clues" said Clair.

"I'll help Alex with Mariam's corpse" said Norman. Everyone else went back downstairs.

Chapter 36

"Where were you planning on looking around at?" Jean asked, as she and Clair walked down the hall.

"I was thinking about Sabrina's bedroom" Clair answered.

"Oh. I'd like to find out what Sabrina is afraid of. That might answer a few questions" said Jean.

"That's one reason why I'm searching. Another reason is about Alice" said Clair.

"Alice? What do you want to know about her?" Jean asked.

"Well, how long have you been working with her?" Clair asked.

"For about a month" Jean said.

"Have you ever noticed anything about her? Anything odd?" Clair asked.

"Now that you mention it, yes. Alice would frequently get strange phone calls and never tell me, Norman, or Mariam about them" said Jean.

"Who do you think was calling her?" Clair asked.

"I'm not sure, but I do know it was a female. I'd sometimes overhear her conversations, but not purposely" said Jean. Clair listened intently. Was it possible the person who called Alice was Sabrina.

"What kinds of things would she talk about on the phone?" Clair asked.

"She'd talk about meeting the person she was talking to in several different places. One time I tried to follow her, but lost her in city traffic. I think she knew I was following, because she disappeared rather quickly. Whoever she was going to meet with, she obviously didn't want me to know" said Jean. Clair was lost in thought. Alice was definitely hiding something.

They soon reached the large double doors of Sabrina's room. They were just as Clair remembered them. The large fancy Ss were still on them. When she turned the handle, it made a grating sound. The gears inside were rusted somehow, probably from years of dust. Jean was amazed by Sabrina's room. The cat pictures, the black concert grand piano, the white canopy bed, the tall grandfather clock. It was all as Clair remembered and dreaded seeing again. These objects all meant Sabrina was still alive. No one ever came into this room except for her. Everything was still shiny and cleaned thoroughly. Sabrina suffered from obsessive-compulsive disorder. Since everything was still clean, that only meant that Sabrina was still alive and returning to LaMore Manor.

"Wow! It's so neat and orderly! I'll bet if Sabrina were here, she'd know exactly where everything is" said Jean admirably. Clair looked at Sabrina's bed and noticed something.

"Sabrina's diary is missing" she said.

"What? You've been here before?" Jean asked.

"Yes. Sabrina always keeps her diary on her bed. Someone took it" said Clair.

"Who would come in here? Certainly not Erika or Gabriella" said Jean.

"What about Alice?" Clair asked.

"I don't think Alice even knows where this room is" said Jean.

"You could be wrong, Jean. I may not be related to Sabrina, but I know she wouldn't leave anything behind or out of place" said Clair.

"What do we do now?" Jean asked.

"There has to be a place where the diary might be easy to find. Maybe in Alice's room" said Clair.

"What if we get caught in her room" asked Jean.

"Maybe you could talk to her and keep her busy while I look around in her room. I've been meaning to look in there anyway" Clair said.

"I'll try and keep her in a different part of the house, maybe in the conservatory wing" said Jean.

"Good. I'll come get you when I'm done" said Clair. They both agreed and went their separate ways.

Chapter 37

Clair opened the door to Alice's room. It was a small guestroom with only one small window. Most of the other guestrooms had two or three windows. It was very simple inside. Just a dresser, bed, some shelves, and Alice's suitcases. Clair decided to look in the dresser first. With no success of anything important, she only found clothes. After searching through the suitcases, she felt like giving up. Alice either knew how to hide things really well or there wasn't anything suspicious about her at all. Clair left the room to go find Jean.

Almost half way to the conservatory, Clair heard her name being called. It was Norman.

"Clair! I'm glad I found you" said Norman, out of breath.

"What?! What's the matter?!" Clair asked.

"There's been another murder" he said.

"Who?!"

"Jean."

Everyone was gathered in the conservatory near Jean's body. She saw Alice crying flippantly. Alexandra and Josephine stood outside the conservatory doors. They had no desire to see a dead body. Clair looked down at Jean's corpse. It wasn't exactly pretty since whoever killed her, decided to do it with a circular saw threw her chest. Jean's blood had been showered everywhere. It was all over the flowers and tiled floor around her. The saw was still in Jean's chest, stuck in a mushy, bloody hole. Clair put her hands over her mouth and turned away, nauseated. Alex pulled her away from the body.

"Alice, did you see what happened to Jean" Clair asked in a shaky voice.

"No, I found her like this" Alice answered.

"What are we going to do about this?! Who is possibly going to die next?!" Hillary shouted in tears.

"Wait a minute. I *told* Jean to go find and talk to you, Alice. How come *you* found her first?" Clair asked.

"I was in the living room. I heard Jean calling for me, so I went and found her here" Alice explained.

"Then, Alice came and told me she had found Jean dead" said Norman.

"Where are we supposed to put *Jean's* body at?" Gabriella asked.

"We put Mariam in the basement. We'll have to put Jean down there too" said Erika.

"Eventually we're going to have to call the police. We can't keep dead people here forever. The basement will start to smell soon" said Harlene.

"I'm well aware of that, Harlene. If you have a better idea, let's hear it" Erika said rudely.

"Yeah, I do. Bury them in the back yard; at least they would have some sort of *proper* burial!" Harlene declared.

"Stop arguing! What we should be most concerned about is *who* is the person that is doing the killing!" Joshua said.

"Who else could have done it?" Norman asked.

"The only people in the house are us" said Gabriella.

"What about Theresa?" Josephine asked as she and Alexandra stepped into the room.

"Yeah, I haven't seen her lately" Alex added.

"I'd like to ask Theresa a few questions…along with Alice" said Clair.

"Why me?!" Alice asked defensively.

"It seems pretty odd to me that my daughter senses something unusual about you. Then, these murders start happening and no one knows why or who is doing them" said Clair.

"You better not be accusing *me* of doing this!" said Alice.

"I am. My daughter doesn't lie, and you may have been crying over Jean's death, but it didn't really seem like you cared" said Clair. Alice gave an expression of hate, but also defense. Everyone was starting to agree with Clair. Alice was feeling out numbered. "I can't really blame you for the deaths. However, from now on you won't be taken lightly" said Clair.

"Go ahead and think however you please. You can't prove anything. These murders are just small things compared to what's probably going to happen in the near future" said Alice with a sly tone. She pushed past everyone and left the room.

Chapter 38

Around five o'clock that evening, Theresa came back to LaMore Manor from spending her day downtown. Erika immediately told her about the second murder and asked if she wanted to leave. Theresa *was* surprised at first, but she had previously told Erika she'd stay and help her get though further times. So, she did. Theresa was almost *too* interested on staying. Erika relayed Theresa's response to Clair.

"That does seem weird. Although, she could just be interested in solving mysteries" said Clair.

"Maybe so. I just thought I'd let you know" said Erika.

"Have you seen Alice lately?" Clair asked. Erika shook her head.

"She hasn't shown her face, but I'm sure she hasn't left either" Erika said.

Later on, around midnight, Clair went to the billiard room to play pool with Harlene. She figured she might as well do something a little entertaining to keep her mind straight.

"Sometimes I wonder what our lives would be like if we never would have met Sabrina" said Harlene as she shot a ball into the left corner hole.

"We wouldn't be in this large haunted mansion right now" said Clair.

"That's for sure" Harlene added. Clair laughed.

"You know, this place really doesn't seem haunted at all" said Clair. She shot a striped ball into one of the side holes.

"Yeah, no haunting has really happened" said Harlene.

"Maybe we should just leave" Clair said.

"Why haven't you, then?" Harlene asked.

"Why haven't *you?*" Clair asked back. Harlene broke up a few solid colored balls. The scattered around the board.

"I guess it wouldn't do any good to just leave. The problem would still be here" Harlene answered.

"I have the same thought. We have to solve this nightmare about Sabrina, otherwise, she'll hunt us until death" said Clair.

"What's her deal anyway? What did we ever really do to her?" Harlene asked. Clair didn't answer. For some reason she stopped playing the game and was looking toward the door.

"Clair? What's wrong?" Harlene asked.

"Did you hear a bang?" Clair asked.

"A bang? No, why do you ask?" said Harlene.

"*I* did. It came from down the hall" said Clair.

"Who could be awake at this hour, everyone's asleep" said Harlene.

"I think I know. We should go take a look" said Clair.

"Alright, but it was probably just the wind blowing tree branches against the windows" said Harlene.

"It not *always* the wind" Clair replied.

The two women ventured out into the darkness of LaMore Manor. It was serene, but had a pessimistic feel to it.

"Where do you want to look?" Harlene whispered.

"Let's head toward the living room" Clair whispered back.

Harlene opened the double doors of the living room. It too, was quiet and murky. The women walked in slowly, looking from side to side cautiously.

"It doesn't seem like anyone's here, Clair" said Harlene. Clair walked further inward with Harlene following. Moonlight glowed through the windows. Clair and Harlene stopped by one of the sofas.

"Well, I guess you right, Harlene. There is no one here" said Clair.

"Let's go back then, this house is scaring me" Harlene said nervously. They turned around and were about to leave until they were suddenly startled by sound. It started in low, and then it started to rise.

"What is that?!" Harlene asked.

"Its music" Clair replied. At the far end of the room, an old gramophone started playing "In the Mood" by Glenn Miller.

"There's definitely someone in here, Clair!" Harlene whispered loudly. They followed the drifting jazz music that flowed rapidly out of the gramophone's horn. Clair was frightened, but also very curious.

"I wonder who started it. Records can't play without the help of a person to start it" said Clair.

"Who's cares! Let's just leave!" Harlene demanded. Instead of stopping the music, Clair began to look around again.

"Something's not right. Do you hear a dripping sound?" Clair asked.

"No, turn off the music" said Harlene. Clair ignored Harlene's request and followed the dripping sound. She discovered it was blood. It was dripping rapidly from an upward area by the windows. Clair and Harlene looked up. Partially hung on one of the drapery rods was Gabriella. The end of the rod was propelled though her neck, allowing her blood to flow freely out.

"Oh god!" Clair cried out. Harlene screamed. The rod was bowing and couldn't hold Gabriella's weight any longer. It broke from the wall and Gabriella's body hit the floor with a loud thud. Clair and Harlene ran out of the room in dismay, not wanting to look back.

Chapter 39

Norman switched on the living room lights. Clair and Harlene had woke every adult and brought them down to the terrible scene they discovered. Norman noticed the gramophone. The record had stopped playing, allowing the needle to run over the same groove again and again.

"Who turned on the gramophone?" Norman asked.

"We don't know, it seemed to turn itself on" said Harlene. Norman flipped the switch and the record stopped spinning. Alex found Gabriella's body. Everyone gathered around her. Gabriella still had a broken part of the drapery rod in her neck. She laid there lifeless with one eye open and the other closed. Norman put his hand over his mouth in shock. Erika started crying and knelt down beside Gabriella.

"How many more people have to die?!" Hillary shouted in distress. She ran out of the room with Joshua following.

"I'll help you clean up this mess, Norman" Alex offered.

"Erika, may I have your permission to search the house?" Clair asked. Erika didn't answer, but nodded solemnly.

"What are you planning on searching for, Clair?" Alice asked.

"Just for history and info" said Clair merely.

The next morning, after breakfast, Clair started her search. Harlene and Alexandra decided to join her.

"First, I'd like to go to the library. The last time we were here, I remember Victor telling me the library had books on the histories of the house and the LaMore family" said Clair.

"Maybe we'll find out something about Sabrina and Eleanor" said Alexandra.

Harlene opened the double doors of the library. The morning light shinned softly through the vast windows. The grandfather clock ticked gently, swinging it's large pendulum steadily. The room was much more comforting during the day.

"Well, where should we start looking? There must be thousands of books in here" said Harlene.

"Every part of the library is organized and marked in sections. Just like a public library" Alexandra pointed out.

"Start looking wherever you want. We need to cover the entire library" said Clair. They all split in different directions. Clair went to the area by the clock, Harlene went to the non-fiction, and Alexandra explored the fiction.

They searched for an hour straight, but didn't find what Clair wanted.

"Keep looking until every book is identified" said Clair. Harlene was losing patience and threw a book in frustration. Alexandra too, was about to give up, when she noticed something different. In the fiction section, between two novels, was a broad red book. On the spine it read *Trigonometry* in bold letters. Knowing the book was non-fiction, Alexandra was puzzled to see it there.

"Harley, come see this" she called.

"What'd you find?" Harlene asked.

"Look at that book, it's a mathematics book"

"So" said Harlene simply.

"*So*, what's it going in the *fiction section*?" Alexandra asked. Harlene stared at the book in confusion.

"Maybe it was misplaced" she said.

"I don't think so, this library is way too organized" said Alexandra. Clair over heard and came over.

"Alexandra's right. Sabrina would never allow a book to stay out of place" she said. Alexandra reached up and pulled the bright colored book off the self. When this happened, the book released a pressure switch and the grandfather clock moved forward, away from the wall on a hidden sliding track. They ran over to the clock to see what it had been hiding. Behind the clock, in the wall, was a small shelf with two books. Clair reached in carefully and took them out. One of the books was Sabrina's diary, which had been missing from her room. The other book was aged, and time had given it frail covers. It was dark green in color and had a lock, which was broken.

"What's this" Clair thought out loud. She brought the books over to the large round table. She opened the green book. On the first page was some cursive writing. It was unable to be read considering the book sat for so many years. Dust had faded the script.

Clair turned a few pages. Not all of the writing was dull, and Clair realized the writing was diary entries. Harlene and Alexandra saw it too. Clair read one of the entries aloud.

November 21, 1893

Today, Percival discovered Innis was stealing from the mansion. I was quite surprised myself. Though, I couldn't care less. I know Innis would never take anything of mine. I wish

Percival could just get along with him. He said he was going to have Innis killed by dawn tomorrow. I wish I could put a stop to this. Although, Percival would be furious if I interfered. He still doesn't know I had an affair with Innis. I'm not going to tell him until the time is right. I'm pregnant now. I'm due in two weeks. I want it to be a boy, and I'm thinking of naming him Jeremiah. Of course, it's Innis' child too. Although, Percival thinks of himself as the father. After Innis' death, I'm going to kill Percival. That way he can stop accusing me of being a witch because of my powers. After his death, he'll be placed in the Butterfly Room. No one will find him there. His skeleton will lay behind Medusa forever. It's perfect.

Patricia Aurelia LaMore

"Um...I guess the LaMore family doesn't have a *bright* history" said Harlene.

"Patricia must be Victor's great grandfather's mother" said Clair.

"She said that Percival will lay behind Medusa forever. What does she mean by that?" Alexandra asked.

"I'm not sure. Medusa was a horrible monster of Greek Mythology. I'm sure you've heard about her in school" said Clair.

"Well, yeah. She was a being that had snakes for hair. And if you looked into her eyes, you'd turn to stone" said Alexandra.

"I'd like to know where the Butterfly Room is. I've never heard of it before" said Clair.

"Well, there are probably many rooms we haven't been in here" said Harlene.

"I just realized something. Patricia named her son Jeremiah. That was also Victor's *father's* name. That would mean that Victor's father was Jeremiah III. Sabrina's powers were passed from Patricia, to Jeremiahs I-III, then to Victor. We already know Sabrina received the traits from Victor" said Clair.

"What about Eleanor?" Harlene asked.

"Eleanor received her pyrokinesis ability from Victor as well. Eleanor's mother was Gabriella. And Gabriella was Victor's sister" said Clair.

"So, Patricia was the main cause of everything" said Alexandra.

"Basically, yes" Clair answered.

"Should we tell anyone else this?" Alexandra asked.

"Maybe just Josh, Alex, Hillary, and Norman. They're the only ones I trust right now besides you two" said Clair.

"Erika probably doesn't know anything about this either" said Harlene.

"Possibly, but I'm not telling her" said Clair.

"We should keep the diaries with us. Someone else might know about the secret compartment too" said Alexandra.

"Alright, I'm going to go search for the Butterfly Room with Harlene. You go find Josephine and keep her company" said Clair. Alexandra did so, and Clair and Harlene started on another investigation.

Chapter 40

Clair and Harlene walked leisurely through the halls. Since the mansion was so large, the Butterfly Room could be anywhere.

"Do you even know where you're going, Clair" Harlene asked.

"Maybe. The Butterfly Room obviously isn't on the first four floors. Most of those rooms are guestrooms. I want to go to the sixth floor" said Clair.

"Well, what about the fifth floor?" Harlene asked.

"No, the sixth. I remember every room on the fifth" Clair replied.

Harlene and Clair reached the sixth floor and stopped. The sixth floor consisted of only one hall with two rows of doors. One of the doors led to the attic. Clair and Harlene remembered the last time they were here. They were running from Sabrina and Eleanor. Now, they felt that feeling again. Or, maybe there was *another* presence in the hall with them.

"Before we go down the hall, let's read another entry from Patricia's diary. Maybe it'll say where the room is exactly" Clair suggested. Harlene *also*, wasn't ready to go down the hall, so she agreed. Clair opened the book and read.

November 30, 1893

I haven't written for a while. I've been busy. Little Jeremiah was born today. Percival immediately thought the baby was his. I finally explained that Innis was the father. Percival was enraged. Even though four days ago he had Innis killed. Percival wanted to get back at him. Since he couldn't, he came after me. I killed him. I poisoned him with alkaline from the conservatory during dinner. He won't bother me ever again. Just like I said before, Percival's body will lay behind Medusa forever. I've made sure the Butterfly Room is securely locked. If anyone try to get in, they'll have to answer the riddle that opens the lock first.

Patricia Aurelia LaMore

"We have to answer a riddle?! I'm terrible at riddles!" Harlene exclaimed.

"Just relax, Harley. *I've* always been good at them. Let's go find out how tricky Patricia LaMore was" Clair said eagerly.

"Why would you want to go see a *dead body?*" Harlene asked sarcastically.

"It's not about that. I *know* there's something more in that room. Patricia put a lock on the door for something else. She could have easily buried Percival in the back yard" Clair explained.

"I think we *shouldn't* open the door. Who knows what *else* is inside" said Harlene.

"My point exactly. Let's go" said Clair. Harlene didn't want to follow Clair anymore, but if she turned back, she might get lost. Harlene took out her cigarette lighter and flicked it on. They needed more light. The long hall only had one window. It was at the far end where the staircase was. They were now heading into darkness.

They looked at every door. It wasn't until at the very end they found the Butterfly Room. There was an old red door, with Butterfly Room written in faded bold letters. Clair reached out and turned the brass doorknob. It wouldn't turn. The door definitely had a lock.

"Well, how are we supposed to know what the riddle is?" Harlene asked.

"I'm not sure. Look around the door for words or something. I'll read some more of Patricia's diary" said Clair. Harlene raised her lighter to the door. Clair looked in the diary and found nothing about the riddle.

"Here's some writing" Harlene said finally.

"What's it say?" Clair asked quickly.

"It says: *I sit in sunlight all day long. I have only one hand, and my face sees the clouds. What am I?*" Clair thought hard.

"What would sit outside all day?" Harlene asked. Clair reread the riddle over and over silently. Harlene did the same. Clair rolled several images of objects through her mind.

"It would have to be something that could be outside every day, and every season" said Harlene. The answer suddenly hit Clair like a freight train.

"A sundial" she said. The brass doorknob suddenly turned with a click, and the door opened partially.

"Of course. A sundial is a clock with only one hand" said Harlene. Clair pushed open the door cautiously. The room was dark. There were no windows.

"Feel around for a light switch" Clair said. Harlene flicked a switch beside her and a small chandelier lit up. Half of the bulbs were burnt out, but it still gave off enough light to see what was inside.

The room was an octagon shape. Many wall trophies were hung up around the walls. In the glass trophy boxes were many different species of butterflies and gypsy moths. They had been captured and put together for display. The room seemed like a little entomology museum. In the center of the room, was a white marble base. On it was a beautiful dark blue vase with butterfly prints on it.

"Wow, I wonder who caught all of these!" Harlene said.

"Maybe Patricia did. She obviously was the only person who knew the riddle's answer" said Clair.

"Well, since she and Innis were so close, maybe they *both* knew about this room. After all, Innis helped build the mansion" Harlene added. Clair agreed.

They both walked around the room and looked at the displays in awe. Harlene was beginning to feel comfortable, until she suddenly found Medusa. She stopped walking and called for Clair. Clair gazed at the Medusa portrait. It was very large. Medusa seemed to be starting at them with a deathly look. Her snake-like tongue was slithering out through her sharp fangs. Her eyes were a bright scarlet color with piercing yellow pupils in the middle. She had long bloody claws that were ready to slice anything into wisps. She indeed had a mass of withering black snakes for hair, seemingly, serpents.

"She looks *really* pissed off" said Harlene. Clair gave a small laugh.

"It's just a picture, Harley. It's made to grab attention" said Clair.

"How do we get behind it?" Harlene asked. Clair saw a small

button beside the portrait and pushed it. The picture opened like a door and revealed a pure dark path behind it.

"Oh…whatever" said Harlene. Clair stepped in with Harlene following.

"I don't know what is down this hall, but we're going to face it together" said Clair boldly.

Chapter 41

Harlene raised her lighter for Clair to see what was ahead of them. Though Harlene was being helpful, the lighter didn't seem to help much.

"The next time I go on an adventure with you, Clair, we're going to stay at a Motel 6" said Harlene sarcastically. Clair heard, but ignored the comment. She knew Harlene was just nervous and making conversation.

As they ventured down the murky corridor, the walls started constricting slowly. Clair and Harlene started to walk partly sideways.

"Are we almost to the end? It's seems like we've been in here for an hour" said Harlene. Clair rounded a corner and saw a door.

"This must be it" Clair said. She opened the door and stepped out of the slender hall. Harlene peered over Clair's shoulder.

"Where are we?" she asked. Clair looked around and recognized the room.

"We're in the music room" said Clair. She was bemused. Harlene stepped out of the doorway, which had been in the wall.

"Well...*that* was entirely pointless!" Harlene said brushing dust off her dress. She shut the lighter. There was now enough light from the large windows. Clair, still confused, began to walk forward throughout the room.

"Why would Patricia have a secret passage from a locked room to *here?*" she asked.

"Maybe she didn't know about it. After all, Victor said Innis made secret pathways in order to steal things" said Harlene.

"True, but she mentioned everything in her diary" Clair said.

"Not really. She only said she put Percival's body behind the Medusa picture. She never said anything about a *passage*" Harlene explained. Clair stopped to think. Something didn't make sense. Maybe the purpose of the passage was to distract them from something. Maybe something back in the Butterfly Room. Clair, after all, could have said correct in thinking Patricia buried Percival somewhere else.

"Clair, what's that sound?" Harlene asked. Clair had been in deep thought and didn't even notice there was a soft melody of music. It flowed through the room like a gentle breeze.

"It sounds like an instrument" said Clair. They looked around the room. It wasn't the piano, it sounded different.

"I think it's a harp" said Harlene. Clair looked toward the far end of the room. Sure enough, a large ebony wood harp was playing. *Playing by itself.* Clair nudged Harlene to look. Harlene was astounded to see a harp playing without a person. Without saying words, the two women walked over to it with curiosity. The harp's strings seemed to move without difficulty. After they came beside it however, it stopped playing.

"I don't like this. I've experienced something like this before" said Clair.

"Do you think Eleanor was playing it?" Harlene asked. Clair looked around uneasily.

"Leave the room" she said quickly.

"What? Why?" Harlene questioned.

"Leave now!"

Harlene was startled by Clair. She started running toward the sliding doors. Clair followed quickly.

"It's a trap!" she yelled as she ran. Harlene reached the doors, which were locked.

"No! I don't want to relive this!" Clair shouted. Harlene motioned for Clair to stop yelling. When Clair did, she realized there was a strange familiar sound. It was a faint sound of energy building up. The large windows of the room were starting to crack rapidly. The sound they were hearing was the same as when Sabrina was about to use her power. Heat started to rise in the room. Clair and Harlene looked over at the windows. Without further warning, the windows shattered into millions of jagged fragments. They flew like a thousand daggers throughout the room. Clair grabbed Harlene and pulled her down to the floor. The flying pieces of thick glass collided with the walls and doors above them. They pierced into the wood like throwing knives. Clair and Harlene both screamed until it was over.

Clair barely wanted to raise her head from the floor. She glanced over at the windows, which weren't windows anymore, except a large opening to the outside. Clair and Harlene felt the wind blowing.

The sliding doors unlocked and opened quickly. Harlene and Clair stood up.

"She's teasing us! The fucking bitch is *teasing* us!" Harlene stammered with anger. Clair also felt fury come over her. She knew Harlene was right. Sabrina or Eleanor just wanted to shake them up a bit now that they were back in the house. They wanted to let them know they were going to finish what wasn't completed. They were now going to come after them, no matter where, or when. Especially when they didn't expect it.

Chapter 42

"Are you sure that this happened to you?" Norman asked when Clair and Harlene told their story.

"Absolutely!" Clair and Harlene said in unison. Everyone was worried after hearing they story, everyone except for Alice and Theresa.

"Of course they're sure! I swear, I can almost *feel* Sabrina and Eleanor's presence!" Hillary chimed in.

"It's okay, mom. We're all scared here" said Josephine.

"*I'm* not scared" said Alice.

"Neither am I" said Theresa.

"Then your both psychotic" said Joshua. Alice shrugged her shoulders and smiled.

"How is it that you two aren't bothered by this?" Erika asked.

"Why do you care?" Theresa asked rudely. Erika stared at Theresa in shock.

"What's the matter with you two?! People had *died* here, and you're acting like nothing has happened!" said Clair.

"Clair, don't raise your voice" said Norman.

"I will if I want to!" She walked directly up to Alice. "I want to know exactly what's going on between you two!" she demanded.

Alice calmly walked away from Clair over toward the liquor cabinet to pour herself some vodka. Theresa stood where she was, folding her arms. Clair felt rage and fought it back.

"What would you say if I told you Eleanor was in the room...*right now?*" Alice asked, pouring the vodka. Clair gave a puzzled look.

"What do you mean?" Alexandra asked.

"You all already know Eleanor died and became a poltergeist. I think it's *fascinating* how she can embody others" said Alice.

"Alice, what's your point?!" Harlene asked in frustration. Clair noticed Hillary had walked over to the fireplace. She was standing with her back facing the crowd. She wasn't saying anything or even moving.

"You're about to find out" Alice answered slyly. "You and Josephine *both* are about to find out." Theresa walked up to Alice and stood with an odd smile.

The room began to feel deathly cold. A strange type of cold that everyone in the room hadn't ever felt before. Alexandra was looking around the room slowly. Josephine walked up to Harlene.

"What does she mean by we'll both know?" she asked with a partial whisper. Harlene didn't respond. She too, had noticed Hillary's unusual action.

"Mom, there's something in here. It's strong, *very strong*" Alexandra said nervously.

"Ally, what's wrong? What is it?!" Clair asked quickly.

"I don't know! It's just so strong!" Alexandra exclaimed as she put her hands on her head. Alex came over to his daughter with Clair. They both held her gently. Alexandra looked as if she were about to faint.

Harlene began to slowly advance toward Hillary, who was still standing like a stone statue. She seemed to be holding something long in front of her. Something thin and black that touched the floor. Almost like a rod.

"Hillary? Hillary, please say something" Harlene said warily.

"Mom?" Josephine asked from behind Harlene. Harlene raised her arm toward Hillary's shoulder. Norman suddenly noticed what was happening.

"Don't touch her!" he yelled. He was too late.

Hillary suddenly turned quickly with a jerk and swung a fireplace poker toward Harlene and Josephine. Both ducked and the poker hit a vase standing calmly on a side table. Hillary's face had a solid, emotionless expression. Her blue eyes were motionless and fixed on Harlene and Josephine. She swung the poker again with swordsman-like movements. The sharp tip barley missed Josephine's head, but grazed Harlene's shoulder.

"Mom, what are you doing?!" Josephine shrieked. Harlene pulled Josephine away when Hillary darted again.

"That's not your mother!" Norman protested. "It's Eleanor!"

Harlene and Josephine ran frantically through the house. Hillary followed them slowly, but surely. She held the poker straight out in front of her.

"How do we stop her?!" Clair asked quickly.

"I don't know! I've never had to deal with this before!" Norman answered. Harlene and Josephine ran into the kitchen and soon found themselves trapped. Hillary opened the door and stared inside. Harlene and Josephine held each other in panic. Hillary entered leisurely. The poker started to catch ablaze. The fire started from the tip and began to creep along the entire rod. As Hillary came closer, Harlene and Josephine could feel the heat of the fire on their skin. Their arm hairs stood up. The fire seemed to take away their breaths. Alexandra snuck into the kitchen. She saw a percolator on the stove, and seized it quickly. Hillary darted once more and Alexandra swung the metal percolator against Hillary's head. The poker missed and stabbed the tiled wall with a harsh cracking sound. Hillary then hit the floor with a thud, with the flaming poker. Harlene and Josephine ran away from Hillary. Norman, Clair, Joshua and Alex came running into the kitchen. Erika stood by the door.

Joshua hugged Josephine, who was crying hysterically. Norman knelt down beside Hillary. Her eyes were open, but only slightly. Norman closed them and took the poker, which had stopped burning, out of her hand.

"You both alright?" Alex asked.

"I'll be okay, but Josie…is really shaken up" said Harlene.

"I'll take Josie upstairs to rest. I can stay with her for a while" said Alexandra.

"You can stay with her, but I would prefer you to stay in the lounge. It's right next to the living room and that's where everyone will be" said Clair.

"Alice and Theresa are still in there" said Erika.

"Good, I want to keep *them* in sight" Clair said crossly.

Chapter 43

Alexandra and Josephine went into the lounge as told, and everyone else came into the living room. Alex and Joshua set Hillary down on one of the sofas. Alice and Theresa still stood by the liquor cabinet. Clair walked in, glaring at them scornfully.

"*Having fun?*" Alice asked sarcastically with a smile. Clair got up in Alice's face with rage.

"*Now* would be the perfect time for you to shut the hell up!" she said dauntingly. Alice still smiled, but didn't respond. Outside, a sudden soft roll of thunder made itself known. Followed by raindrops hitting the windows.

"Both on you, from now on, are not allowed to be left alone" said Norman.

"Just how are you going to pull that one off?" Theresa asked rudely.

"They're not. You see, Clair, Sabrina *is* in the house. And thanks to Theresa and I, she can finally get even with you" Alice said.

"You keep saying that, but not yet proven it" Alex said.

"*Prove it!* I don't have to *prove* it. The murders should have told you that" said Alice.

"I don't believe Sabrina is responsible, Alice" said Joshua.

"Josh is right. You killed Jean and Mariam! Didn't you, *Alice?!*" said Clair.

"And Gabriella too" Erika added.

"I didn't kill Mariam, or Gabriella. Although, I had the perfect moment for Jean when she came to tell me about the secret compartment you found in the library" Alice confessed.

"Which, by the way, is *no* secret" Theresa added.

"Then who killed the others?!" Clair asked impatiently.

"Eleanor of course" said Theresa.

"Come forth, Eleanor. Make yourself known" Alice said, looking around the room. She had her hands raised in the air.

Alexandra and Josephine looked in from the lounge.

"What are you trying to do?" Alex asked.

"I'm just bringing out an old friend" Alice said, and she called for Eleanor again.

"This is ridiculous. I'm going to call the police. We should have gotten them a long time ago" said Norman. He started walking toward the telephone. Alice took out a revolver from her pocket and aimed it at Norman. She then pulled the trigger and Norman fell down to the floor in alarm.

"Oh!" Erika exclaimed fearfully. She and Joshua immediately knelt down beside him. He had been shot in his upper side and the bullet had ripped through his heart. Erika was trying to stop the bleeding with her sweater vest.

"There's no point on trying now…he's dead" said Joshua. Erika looked at Joshua in sorrow an slowly stopped applying pressure to Norman's side.

"We can't have the police here. I *might* go to jail" said Alice, in a psychotic concerned tone. Clair dove toward Alice in anger, and Alice raised her gun at Clair briskly.

"Hold it, chicky! I'm not ready for *you* to die yet!" she said. Alex pulled Clair away from the gun. Clair still glared at Alice in fury.

"What do ya think, Theresa, should I shoot her, or let Sabrina do the job?" Alice asked. When Theresa spoke, her voice slowly changed into a very familiar one. One that anyone could never forget once they've heard it.

"I think they've been warned by you enough. Besides, who better to kill them than...*myself*" she said horridly. By this time, Hillary had woken to her normal self. Everyone but Alice looked at Theresa in surprise. Theresa's brown eyes started to become a vibrant green. Like the celadon green of a cat's eye. They knew right away that Theresa was not who she seemed to be. As she slowly transformed into another person, Alice spoke up.

"I'd like everyone to welcome my dear friend...*Sabrina*" she said.

Chapter 44

Clair backed away from Sabrina and Clementine slowly, with widened eyes. Alexandra and Josephine looked in with awe.

"So...that's Sabrina" Alexandra said to herself. Erika stood up quickly.

"Not again, Sabrina! You don't have to hurt us!" she exclaimed. Sabrina looked at Erika.

"Quiet, mother. You have no say here" Sabrina said dully.

"Please, Sabrina! I'm your mother!" Erika said.

"I know" Sabrina replied with a ghastly tone.

The lights in the room dimmed slowly as Sabrina glared sourly at her victims. Beside her, a ghostly appearance of Eleanor appeared. She hovered delicately with a fixed expression of wrath. Her skin was a eerie white color, and she had dark glowing eyes with silvery pupils. The room became deathly cold, and ice formed on the floor around the bottom of Eleanor.

"You see, Clair, you run...and you run...but you can't get away" Alice whispered. Her hand trembled slightly as she held the gun. Alexandra snuck into the room and made her way behind

Alice. Josephine caused a distraction by running over toward Hillary.

"Calm down, Alice. You're too tense" Clementine said. Alice let out a deep breath and wiped sweat off her forehead.

"I'm fine" she responded. Everyone noticed Alexandra, but didn't look at her, since they feared Sabrina or Eleanor would see them looking.

Eleanor wasn't speaking. It soon occurred to everyone that she couldn't. She was only able to float there and glare with haunting hatred. Although, if looks could kill, Eleanor's would be fatal.

Alice was too overexcited to hold the revolver correctly. She kept switching her aim from one person to another. She couldn't make up her mind on who to kill next.

"Give Sabrina the gun, Alice. You're obviously too edgy" said Clementine.

"Stop it! I can handle this gun just as well as *you* can!" Alice snapped. Sabrina shifted her anger toward Alice. The gun flew out of Alice's hand and then aimed itself at her. "What are you doing, Sabrina?! I'm your friend!" Alice exclaimed. Eleanor smiled atrociously. She, among several others, knew you should never go against Sabrina's demands.

"It's time for you to make a decision now, Alice. Do you want to live…or die?" Sabrina asked. Alice was very frightened.

"Clementine! Don't listen to her! Sabrina is only going to control you!" Alice yelled. Everyone but Eleanor was shocked. Erika walked up to Clair and Alex.

"Do you realize what Alice is talking about?" she asked.

"No" Clair said in confusion.

"There is one thing about Sabrina you don't know" Erika said. Clair thought carefully and was completely puzzled.

"I have a thought" Alexandra said slowly. "Sabrina's real name isn't *Sabrina*...its Clementine." A clash of thunder and lightning struck the sky. Clair knew now. Sabrina and Clementine weren't just the same person.

"Sabrina has Dissociative Identity Disorder. Which means, Sabrina's other personality is Clementine" said Clair.

"Except, Sabrina is mostly the dominant personality, and the evil one. Clementine is who my daughter really is. She's the gentle one, the *real* one. Clementine is my *true* daughter" Erika explained.

"You knew this all along?!" Clair asked angrily.

"Yes" Erika said.

"The only way to save Clementine is to kill Sabrina!" Alice shouted.

"I've had enough of you!" Sabrina growled. She pulled the trigger of the revolver and the bullet rushed into Alice's head. Alice flew against the wall. She slid slowly down to the floor, leaving a blood trail on the wall. The bullet had gone through her head. Everyone suddenly grabbed the chance to leave. They quickly ran for the front doors. Sabrina didn't run after them. She simply followed gradually, since she could always catch them.

"We can't kill Sabrina! If we do that, will also kill Clementine!" Alexandra shouted as they ran.

"Ally's right, they share the same body!" Clair said. They reached the doors and flung them open. The rain storm outside was brutal. Erika shouted for everyone to stop running.

"Why?! She'll catch us!" Alex said.

"Just trust me!" Erika answered. Sabrina slowly surfaced out of the dark in the hallway. She suddenly stopped and just stood at the front entrance. She had an extreme look of worry on her pale face. Everyone, but Erika, was surprised.

"Sabrina *does* have a fear" said Erika. Clair, being well educated, realized Sabrina's phobia.

"She has Ombrophobia…she's afraid of the rain" she said.

"We're safe!" Hillary exclaimed. "Sabrina won't come out here!" The rain was pouring down heavily. Sabrina was furious. She immediately threw her victims backwards with a strong force of telekinesis. She picked up the Dellers' little Chevette and threw it at them. Everyone, however, had enough time to get out of the way, before the car hit the ground.

"You won't kill us Sabrina! Clementine won't let you!" Clair yelled.

"You're a fool, Clair! Clementine is too weak to surpass *me*!" Sabrina shouted back. Next, she threw Alice's station wagon. It too, missed her victims and landed beside them.

"Clementine, try and come out! You can do it!" said Erika.

"No she can't!" Sabrina yelled. "I am all who exists…Clementine is gone!" Everyone started to encourage Clementine to come out. They called her name over and over.

"Stop it! Shut up!" Sabrina snarled in anger. Clementine was suddenly getting stronger. Sabrina gasped, and held her head. She dropped Clementine. "No! I won't let you come out! You need me!" Sabrina said.

"No! You're evil! And evil has to die!" Clementine shouted out. Josephine was too scared to look. She covered her eyes and Hillary and Joshua hugged her. A strong wind was blowing wildly. The windows of LaMore Manor shattered with great force. The ground shook immensely as large cracks fissured through it. Everyone could hardly stand.

"Stop it, Clementine! You need me! I'm your protector!" Sabrina commanded.

"Not anymore!" Clementine said. Sabrina and Clementine's body flew out into the rainstorm. The ground in front of the mansion collapsed. Clair watched as the ground pulled Sabrina and Clementine down into the earth. There was a flash of light as the rocks and dirt covered their body. Clair and all her friends and family were thrown backwards again, and landed on the ground. They all laid there unconscious as the storm started to die.

Chapter 45

By the next morning, the sky was clear and the sun was shining. Everyone had been awakened by police and medical technicians. In front of LaMore Manor, lay a giant sinkhole. Everyone thought Clementine had killed Sabrina. Clair, however, knew better. She remembered the flash of light, just before Sabrina had disappeared into the ground. She knew…Sabrina was still alive.

There really is no happy ending to this story. Clair, and her family, are living peacefully now. So is Joshua's family, and Harlene and Maximilian. Erika moved away. She moved far away from most civilization to the high north of Canada. As for Eleanor, she still remains in what is left of LaMore Manor.

Its late autumn now. New York City is busy, just like always. Snow hasn't fallen yet, but…it just started. Soft white flakes of ice are coming down serenely all over the city. On the top of the Statue of Liberty, on the torch, Sabrina stands there in content with her arms raised slightly. Her eyes are closed and her doll is beside her. This is how it's going to be. Sabrina will eventually catch Clair. She has stopped chasing the others. She won't harm her, or even test her anymore.

Another part of this story I failed to mention, but I'll tell you now. Sabrina has a good reason for wanting to talk to Clair. When Clair was born, her father wasn't around. Clair was raised from a single parent until her mother remarried. Her original father disappeared. Before Clair though, was another child. A child that was taken away by Clair's first father. Sabrina just needs to tell her… "I'm your sister."

Author's Notes

My inspiration for this book had actually started years ago. Sabrina Eileen LaMore, was created when I was in my early teen years at age fourteen. I've always loved to write, and my family has always been a dedicated support for me. I finished "Sabrina" at age seventeen, and I'm currently in my twenties now. However, I am also currently working on a prequel to this novel. I have written other novels, and gotten positive praise from my readers. With publication of my books, I hope to gain a much larger audience. Rest assured, I have more books on the way.

Scott M. Stockton

CPSIA information can be obtained at www.ICGtesting.com
Printed in the USA
BVOW05s1014020714

358018BV00001B/39/P

9 781448 983926